TIME-LESS VOICES-BEFORE I FALL ASLEEP

A COMPILATION OF POEMS AND SHORT ESSAYS
VOLUME I and II

TIME-LESS VOICES- BEFORE I FALL ASLEEP

A COMPILATION OF POEMS AND SHORT ESSAYS
VOLUME I and II

JANETHA S. PIERPOINT

CITI OF BOOKS

For permission requests, write to the publisher, addressed "Attention: Permissions Coordinator," at the address below.

CITIOFBOOKS, INC.
3736 Eubank NE Suite A1
Albuquerque, NM 87111-3579
www.citiofbooks.com
Hotline: 1 (877) 389-2759
Fax: 1 (505) 930-7244

Ordering Information:

Quantity sales. Special discounts are available on quantity purchases by corporations, associations, and others. For details, contact the publisher at the address above.

Printed in the United States of America.

ISBN-13:   Paperback   979-8-89391-142-8
              eBook   979-8-89391-143-5

Library of Congress Control Number: 2024910158

The following are descriptions of my personal experiences and provocative pieces of work presented through the extension of poems and essays, including the expression of artwork. I am excited to introduce you to the visionary work of Time-Less Voices—Before I Fall Asleep. This collection extends beyond traditional artistry, encompassing a rich venue of poems, essays, and expressive artworks. Each piece is a journey into the depths of imagination and introspection, inviting you to explore the interconnectedness of mind, body, and spirit.

Time-Less Voices—Before I Fall Asleep merges the digital realm with traditional artistry, crafting pieces that resonate with the soul. Through meticulous strokes and profound connections to the Universe's rhythms, this author/artist creates visual poetry that transcends language and captures the essence of existence.

As you, the audience, venture into this collection, you will encounter narratives woven with threads of emotion, inviting you to embark on a journey of self-discovery and introspection. Each artwork, poem, and essay reflect the artist's profound understanding of life's beauty and complexities.

As the author, I invite you, the reader, to immerse yourself in this visionary work, where art, poetry, and essays converge to provoke thought, inspire and awaken new perspectives.

CONTENTS

AUTHOR'S NOTE

Let the reader acknowledge that all works in this volume are about my experiences. My direct and indirect experiences, along with her observations of others' life experiences, have taught me lessons.

The information contained herein is factual, about my life. It is not intended to distract from the truth; therefore, I am not liable for misrepresenting my own experience. I am not to be held liable for any misunderstood words or for my own eyewitness accounts.

In this work, I write of the behaviors of others. I will never unlearn the verifiable facts of my life experiences and will never forget those involved in certain episodes. What my ears have heard and what my mind since has analyzed will remain the truth.

Therefore, neither I nor the publisher assumes any responsibility for how the reader perceives these words or any opinions readers may have about the subject matter. This work is educational and is forthcoming about the experiences I have had while journeying through life. This work is not intended to cause mayhem or unsettle emotions, but to educate others to look deeper and find support for their concerns.

I am not to be called prejudiced based on any negative emotions the reader may feel. I do not grant interviews or have any desire to be summonsed for litigation. There will be no discussion about my personal life, in disaccord, as I will tell my readers and those with curious minds to respect these writings and support humanity by doing what matters.

The publisher of this work shall have no responsibility or authority to provide my address, make suggestions, give advice, or express any opinion on my writings. I and publisher have a fiduciary relationship for the purpose of publishing and selling this work.

Therefore, in regard to any materials and products, in no event shall I or the publisher be liable for any direct or indirect, incidental, punitive, or consequential damages whatsoever related to this written material or the other products such as artwork.

I respect the rights (including the intellectual property rights) of others, and I ask my readers and any curious seekers to do the same. I may, in appropriate circumstances, and under my sole discretion, advise readers not to infringe on or otherwise violate the rights of others.

All information herein is shared with good intentions. There is no guarantee of any kind made, expressed, or implied regarding the completeness, accuracy, adequacy, validity, reliability, or availability of any information herein.

PREFACE

Starting from the beginning, or what I remember as the beginning, I will share the story of my life, but first I will share the middle part, during which I endured some harsh challenges. That period came amid unexpected forces, manifesting a mix of experiences that, I guess, led me to become the person I am today. Am I answering any questions? No. Although I am not hiding under a rock, I would like to share that I started out as a displaced child because others initially left me behind, leaving me to try to figure things out on my own as time moved forward.

Coming from a somewhat humble background, but not one of defeat, I withstood those things that challenged me. I will not share these details to put things into perspective because I do not want to stress any younger readers. I will give the hint that through the poetry presented and the other types of work herein, one will find an introduction to my life.

However, I will share that, like many of the roads many of us travel down, the road I've traveled along life's journey has been one with bumps, letdowns, hardships, heartbreaks, disappointments, shame, and insecurity, which most times depleted my strength. These things came about through negligence, abuse, pain, torture, and repeated lacerations, leaving me with scars in my earlier years, both those that tattooed my body and those that troubled my mind. Also, I share my lack of proper education, having been miseducated, which exacerbated the struggles that continued to test me as time wore on.

Remembering that life is not always fair, whether we want to entertain that notion or leave it behind, I conclude that there really is no room for losers. Either a person has the encouragement and commitment to get up and make a difference, or a person does not. There is no room for those who complain or whine about what they should have done or not have done. We each reach a point where we want to exchange the cards that we have been dealt. Getting what we need out of this life is solely up to us.

Yes, I could sit and tell of my flaws, share my outcomes, and tell of the many mistakes I failed to learn from. I could also tell of how others hindered me in my life. Some people have hated me all my life. I used to blame myself for things I had insufficient knowledge to address, while working on the things I felt I needed to learn.

I could share that the sea of depression rose above my head, and it took a toll when I learned I could not have children, through no fault of my own. At my mature age, I am still trying to complete this mission, even considering other alternatives. Giving up is not part of my makeup, and I will not allow age to prevent me from being a mother to someone. For this reason, I will keep pushing myself until I cannot go any farther.

One promising about my life is that I share it with my husband, who is known by family and friends as a dedicated and committed person who will take a stand for me, who honors our relationship, and who does his due diligence to help achieve the dreams that he and I share.

Let me not forget to mention that as a husband, he does not hold back from telling me the truth. He says exactly how he feels about any projects I present to him to edit. Yes, I need his opinion. It helps me stay humble, so that I can get the work done. I learned quickly how to hold my tongue, which has helped me to be a better team member. I also now know the importance of delegating tasks.

Now, I stand here to say that I can only admire the effort my husband puts forth and the commitment he shows, knowing he has to complete that which needs to be finished. So, I tell him morning, noon, and evening, and throughout the night, "I love you, and I thank you."

Suppose you should ask what inspired me to write the things that I have written. Many points in my life brought me to this place, starting with the many experiences I learned from but hadn't given my attention to that aided in my personal development. However, the one thing that gave me a greater awareness was the attention I paid to the circle of life and death and all the in-betweens, including the interactions played out on life's stage. Further, I attest that writing has been therapeutic for me, helping me to release any toxicity that had accumulated over time. This action played a role in healing my mind and distributing positive energy to my soul.

I seek to live a life worth living, using my intelligence to become the person I want to be. I seek to find a higher mission as I continue this journey toward greater self-development. I honor the need to focus on my duties, ensuring I engage in constructive work. I must be disciplined in this life to give as much as I can give, and I adhere to the law of having unconditional love for myself and others.

I need a clearer understanding of those higher connections, such as to my ancestors and their present vibrational energy, which is connected to me. I have a passion for reaching out to others, sharing, and teaching anyone who cares to listen as I travel along my path. While on this journey to develop my cosmic being, I seek out numerous people to get their advice and assistance.

I need to enhance my creativity and intuition so I can better tap into scientific principles and become more clairvoyant, thereby knowing more. I want to download information about many things into my consciousness so that it may be beneficial to my work. One must embrace life and that which needs to be manifested if one wishes to have a continuous flow of love to transfer to others.

Many people I have come across in my travels have asked me what I believe is essential. It takes me no time to answer. I share that I focus on stability, saying that I am not able to get myself to a better place without using the strength that helps me keep my balance. Without maintaining focus and balance, I would be displaced. Balance is essential to fulfilling my mission. I want more from this life, desiring stability. I stand on the principle that one should not limit one's life to what others assign one to. Life offers an abundance—and it starts with you.

As you read my written reflections, I ask to free your soul's energy of any negative connections by saying out loud: "I am done with any negativity that may bring harm to another or bring about any affliction in my life. I am done with allowing others to control me. I do not consent to any theft of my soul's energy. I release myself from any contracts that hold me in bondage."

ACKNOWLEDGMENTS

I owe much appreciation and gratitude to my husband, my life partner, Victor Pierpoint, who not only contributed to and enhanced the work in these volumes but also dedicated his time without knowing in advance that his commitment would never end. I am also grateful for the insights and support of family, such as my sister, Dirisha Zuri, who helped with research, and my auntie Beu Brown, who did some research on various topics. Also, much thanks to a multitude of friends, such as James Mort, a professional consultant, and Ra Griffith, who provided an honest critique of this work. Then, a host of others gave me their support, including former colleagues and professionals, who indirectly inspired me. I also give thanks to Fane Khan for being very encouraging and giving me her professional advice when building my website.

I personally thank my grandparents for their support and for shaping me into the person I am today. My grandparents have since made their transition.

I give thanks for the motivation I have to push forward and honor my daily commitment to stay focused, as without such focus, I never would have finished this project.

I continue to thank my husband and others for sitting and listening to these works and for reading me books on various subjects—poetry, reflections, essays, and so forth. I'll throw in that they all claimed to have enjoyed giving their input.

Approach each piece herein with attention, considering the thoughts and ideas discussed.

Since taking on this life mission, I have been inspired to push forward and have been empowered to write, create, and help to enlighten others.

I want to give thanks to those who are members of the global family. Perhaps you will become followers of this work. Furthermore, I would like to thank everyone in advance for their engagement with these words, which have their beginnings in my imagination. In return, I will commit to my purpose in life and will remain inspired to continuing creating and sharing. I am forever indebted to you all.

TIME-LESS VOICES

BEFORE I FALL ASLEEP

JANETHA S. PIERPOINT

INTRODUCTION

When speaking about patience, time management, leadership, and workmanship, there is no better example than my husband, Victor Pierpoint. Victor proves his high caliber by working until the work is done. I would describe him as showing the essence of commitment, a man who fine-tunes his tools before applying his knowledge and skills. I cannot say it enough that Victor needs to be honored for his craftsmanship, stamped with his passion and artistry. Any person would race to him have on their team.

This is the blueprint of my project, the launch of my thoughts and ideas. I will admit that speaking to Victor about developing a website; writing books, scripts, and reflections; doing drawings; and facilitating the continuous flow of creative ideas made for some of the most tedious work. This initially made him pull back from participating. He stood wondering what I had exposed him to, asking, "Would someone please tell me, who on earth did I marry?" If you had seen the look on his face, you would never forget it. I let him know that a woman will never tell her husband everything. This is called the art of allowing a man to get to know you. Many men appreciate this type of connection that grows over a lifetime.

Victor was blindsided when he learned what the project would entail. He did not realize that he would have to do research and editing, using his mental capacity to tidy up my ideas. He had to forget about complaining about being too tired to complete the task, as this was not part of the agreement.

Later, Victor learned the meaning of the word *mission*, moving forward and making a lifetime commitment. With no end in sight to my assignment, I will only continue to thank Victor until we are no more. I give him my appreciation for not counting me out, not folding on my ideas, and not defining me as a delusional dreamer who failed to put in the work. I appreciate him for his time and his dedication while journeying with me through life.

Volume I

CELEBRATION OF A PROMOTION

Today we celebrate your promotion in life, and we celebrate with you—your new position in life after identifying your life purpose. We appreciate the efforts you have made in striving to aim high. All along, you continued with your mission as you journeyed through time.

So much has been given to you, and there is so much more for you to receive in life. For those who care not and those who choose to stay on the sidelines, not appreciating others' accomplishments, let them remain seated.

You should never be suspended in time, wondering if someone else cares or not, as you should be spared from doing work, and you should be allowed to move on with your journey.

Remember, patience is one of your best teachers, and life lessons are your master teachers, but perseverance is the energy that helps you breathe with purpose.

Don't dare let your heart worry about any of this, as looking into the rearview mirror will cause you to lose focus.

Stop questioning if the recognition of others matters when recording your good deeds. Embrace the energy that comes with knowing that your efforts to serve humanity are a staple in your life. Your hard work will be rewarded by the growth of your soul.

Do not be concerned about others who attempt, with false accusations, to hold you accountable for things you do not do or know not know of.

Practice the art of distancing yourself from others who fail to honor you or respect who you are, people who instead criticize the good deeds that you do in service to humanity.

Recall the time you have been given, and do not deliberately waste it on things that should not matter. And don't intentionally show disregard for another's valuable time.

If you fail to value your time, you will cause the time you have to be measured while ignoring any time manifested for you.

Let go and allow life to create while you are answering your call. Remain ready to promote growth by giving your support to those who could use it.

Today we toast you, a special person on a new mission to make cosmic waves, moving forward to continue creating life.

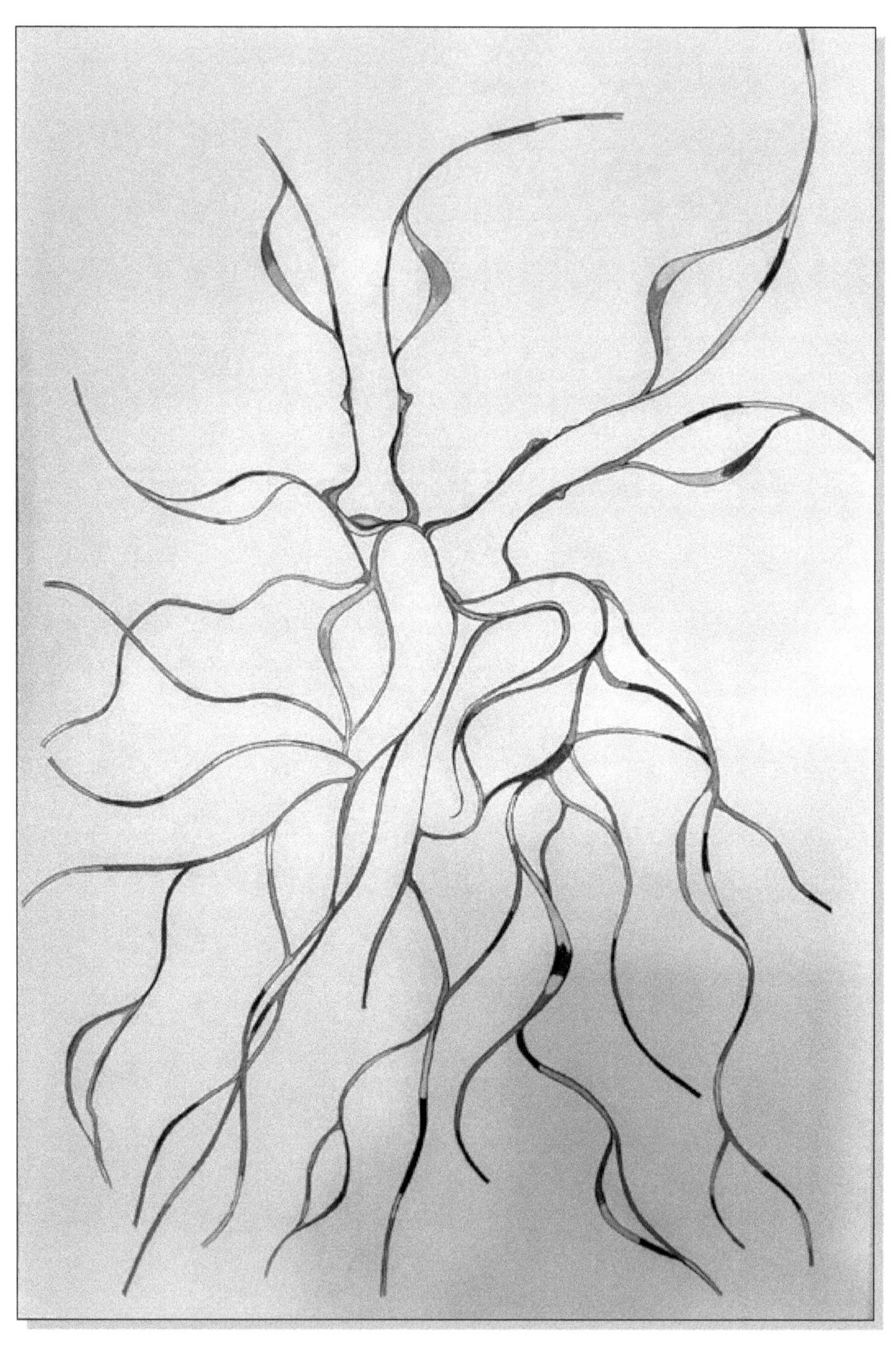

ONE MORE THING I NEED TO SAY

Today I would like to take a little time to thank you for all the beautiful things that you have brought into my life.

It brings me joy and happiness to be your wife. I cannot find the words to express it. I thank you for your love and for your precious thoughts and feelings that reach my spirit and then touch it.

I honor your dedication as a husband and your commitment to me, your wife. You keep uplifting me, which teaches me not to overborrow from people I appreciate, as this way I stay thirsty for more. The ways in which you uplift me feed my blood, generating positive energy within my cells.

Like my husband, I have learned to be healthy while still being a student of life. I am determined to move ahead, putting my best foot forward, serving a purpose. I came to do what I need to do while continuing to create and to love you as the beautiful soul you are.

You are the light being that comforts me and protects me. I cannot stop expressing this fact. You know that our love will remain.

When I see you, I am embraced by your soul.

I give appreciation to Anu, creator of the universe, for answering my request to have a "genie" stationed in my life. I show gratitude to my partner, who knows who he is and does not shy away from being an honorable man.

For these reasons, I dedicate the flow of my breath to you whom I breathe right along with. Although I may not have been there during your arrival into this world in this physical form, I will remain right here until you depart from this plane of physical existence and go to the place of spiritual consciousness.

Today, we arrive together at this appointed time and in this appointed space to continue to work and build with each other.

For love shared and for shared sincerity, I thank the universal consciousness within me, but I also vow to marry my husband spiritually every day.

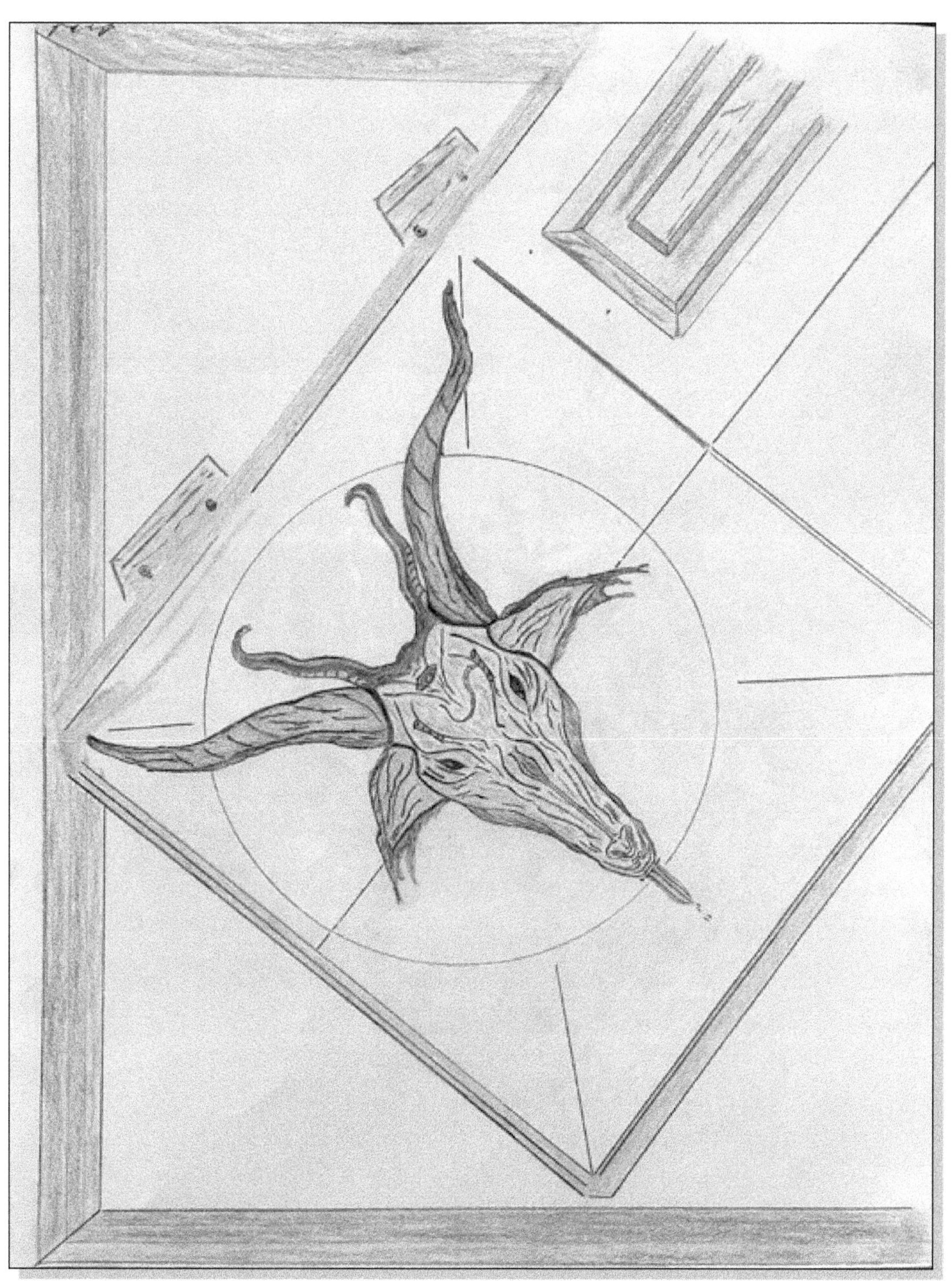

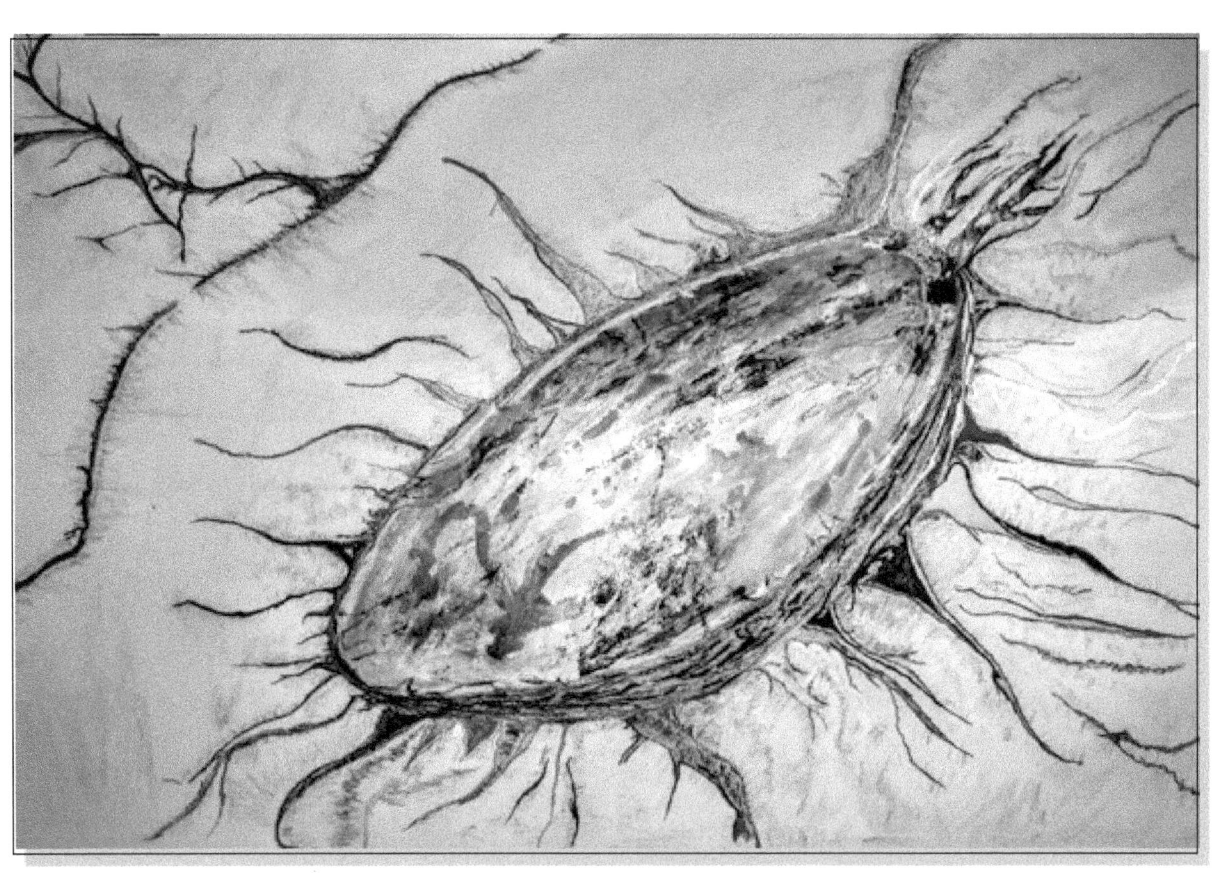

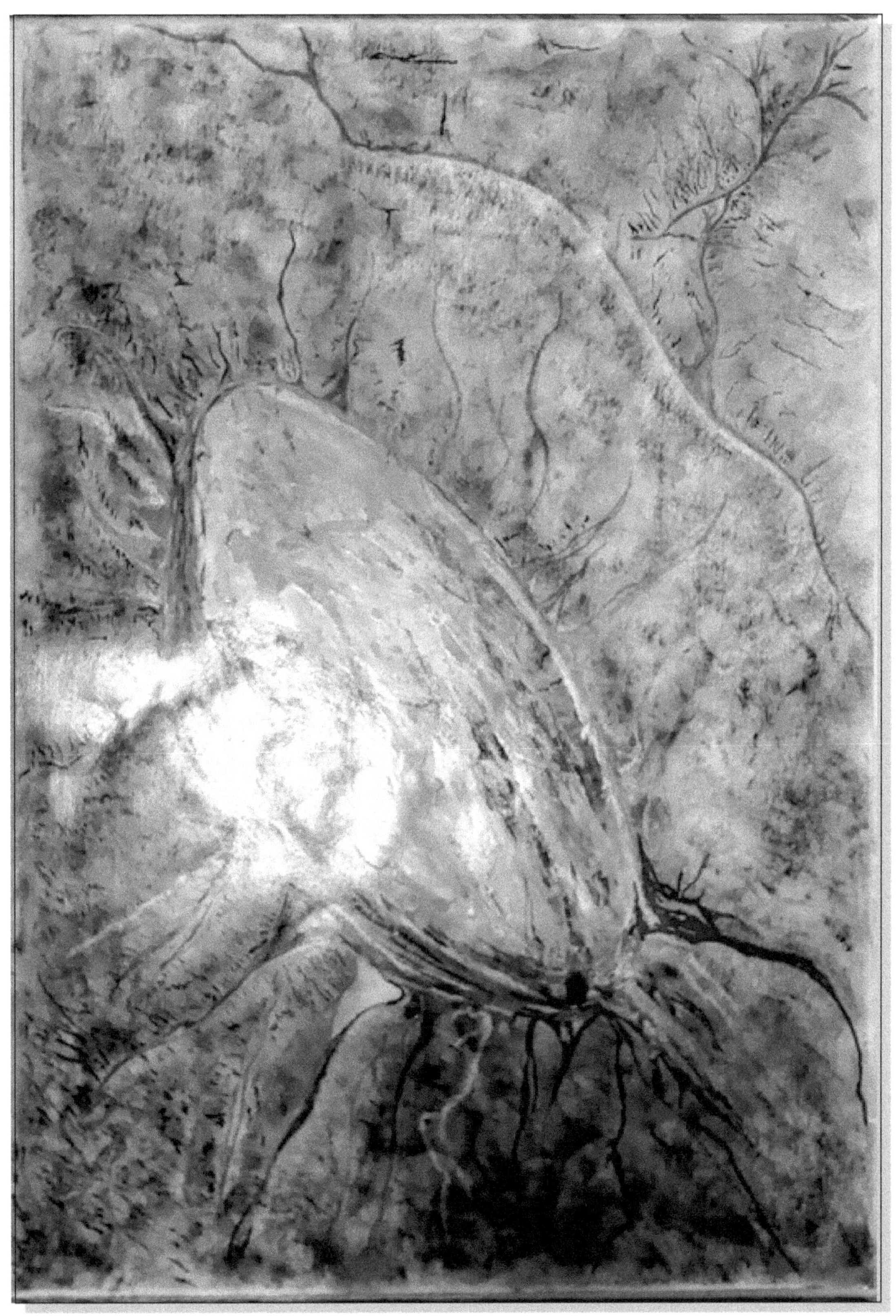

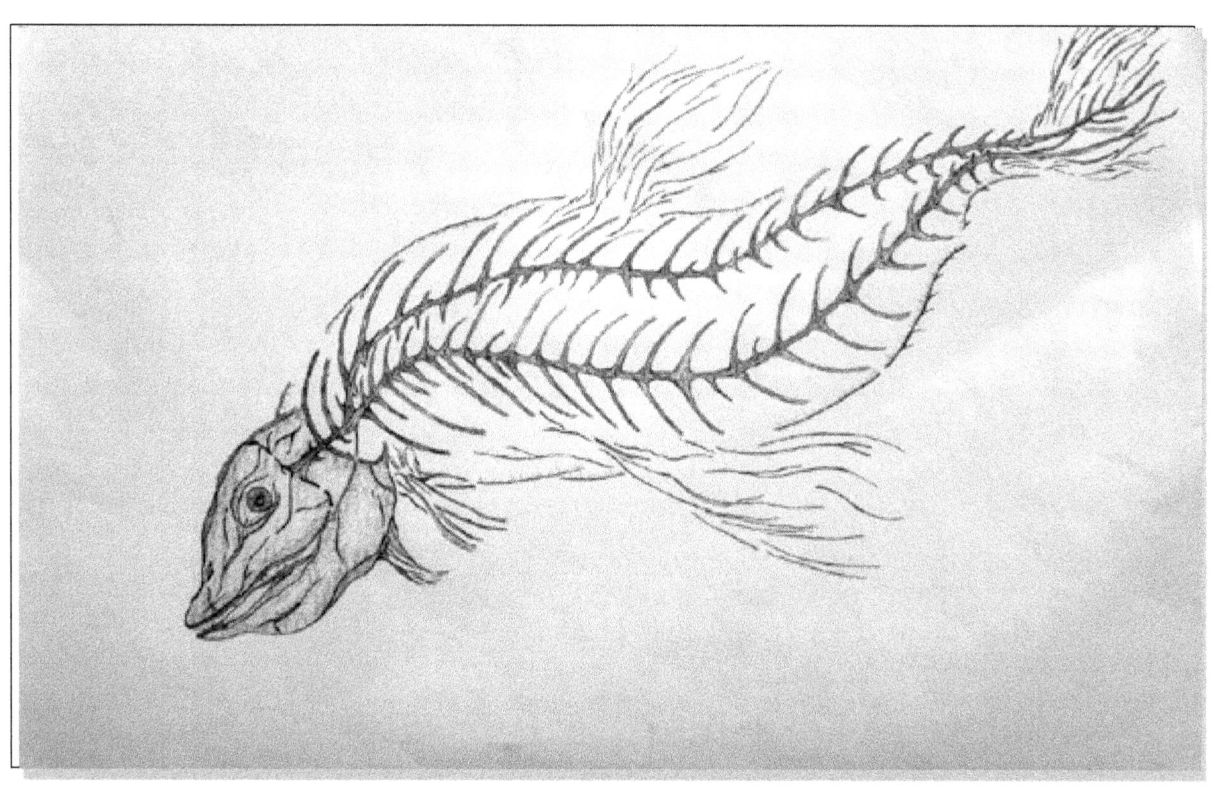

A TRIBUTE IN HONOR OF EXCELLENCE

I have heard it said that the actions of a man speak louder than his words. Surely, if you want to assess a man's real character, then pay less attention to what he says and more attention to what he does.

Today, we honor a colleague. I am confident that everyone who has worked with him in his thirty-five years here would agree that he is an outstanding individual who seems to take pleasure in helping others by sharing the expertise gained from his many years on the job.

On this day, we honor and praise William for his accomplishments and for serving our organization. A review of his exceptional service history shows that he has been a dedicated member of our team, taking on additional responsibilities and supervising others, even overseeing those who were not under his authority.

His résumé listing his many assignments speaks for itself. There is no end to what he can do while continuously learning.

I asked William, when wondering about his responsibility for supervising so many people, "Are their different personalities a challenge for you?"

He stared at me and smiled as he usually does when I ask him a question. With the same smile, he answered, "We all have our unique personalities," and left it at that. I walked away thinking about his comment, concluding, *He sure has a great universal personality.*

Listen, it gets better. William's career with this organization continued with his being a dedicated worker. He continued to use his artistry as related to his profession when he was made a supervisor. After several reassignments in his later years, William was given a position involving the mentoring of others.

Later he was repeatedly assigned to teach and mentor, and he carried on with this task until he grew weary. He wondered if he still had it in him to keep doing what he believed was his life's work to help others. This question was answered when he was promoted, not just to supervise staff, but also to oversee management.

It was not until one of his last assignments that I met William. It didn't take long before I came to know him and understand his quirky ways. I began to like him as a person, not only because of his winning smile, but also because he is a unique individual who expresses genuine concern for his work.

Both I and my many colleagues appreciate William a great deal. As a committed employee, he should be acknowledged for the strength he brings to this organization, as he has helped to grow another's empire.

He is respected, appreciated, and acknowledged by his colleagues. We commend him for mastering all the tasks he performed for the organization, for his artistry, for his dedication to his many assignments, and for a job well done.

If you want to know what type of person William is, well, you don't have to go far to find out. He is a man of expertise who strives for perfection. And although his highest aim is to continue working and achieving, William's secret weapon for becoming better is to make himself available to his colleagues and provide service to the community at large.

The word is that William has proven himself to be a loyal, dedicated, hardworking person who shines in many a situation and, according to many accounts, helps others with their daily assignments.

I will give one example, although there are many to choose from. One time I asked William for his help to gather information. Although he did not know me well, as I was not under his authority, he happily assisted me without hesitation.

To speak of William's depth, I will use poetry, which may help to form a more personal connection and better describe our colleague:

> I have heard it said that the actions of a man
> are the things he causes to come true, things that help him to
> develop character and strength for use in each project he pursues.
>
> His efforts to stoke up his strength cause him to make the strides he'll need
> to fly. William gets pleasure from helping people like you and me.

William, if you think you have not been heard,
not been acknowledged,
not been appreciated,
not been honored,
not been admired for your expertise,
not been admired for your strength and commitment,
and not been praised for all the great qualities you have developed—

(Pause. I am a little out of breath, but I must continue)—

then know you are wrong. And although this is the least we could say about
such a great colleague and friend (we could use many more words to sing
your praises),

today we salute you, honor you, and say thank you for your dedication
today and tomorrow.

We stand at attention and tip our hats to you in appreciate of all that you
have accomplished. You have shown that you have the ability to improve
others' lives.

PAYING TRIBUTE TO STAFF WHERE WE STAND COLLECTIVELY AS ONE IN UNITY AND MUTUAL SUPPORT

Time dwindled when I referred to the person I had chosen to shine a light on, my having nominated a single individual. I backed up in my thoughts, only to find myself reading again and again the words of the email, specifically, two words, *accomplishment* and *exemplary*.

At first, my intuition told me to observe a moment of silence, then it said to me, *Wait, don't go there. Leave it to another to make the final decision as to who most deserves to be acknowledged in what category.*

Anxious as I was, I couldn't wait. Time was not on my side. The nominations had to be submitted by October 20, 2020, no later than four o'clock in the afternoon. Thinking about how best to serve my colleagues, I had to make a quick decision and present an essay to help them understand.

Sadly, in defeat, or so I thought, I challenged myself repeatedly, only to rise late at night, bothered, aggravated, and worried about who most deserved the award. *Could it be me?* I wondered. *After all, I work hard, and I challenge myself.* But in the end, I declined to nominate myself.

I shall not rush with a decision.

After hounding myself to make a decision, you see, I gave it more thought and realized in a jiff that to nominate myself would be to highlight only my own achievements and not those of others. Others would judge me and, dare I say, talk behind my back, expressing their concerns—and it would probably only end up as a matter of office politics.

So, I stopped myself from retreating to a corner where I could be in solitude. Again, I challenged my thinking and realized that the only time when one is given logic is when one is resolving madness. Who most deserves an award may not be the right question. Sometimes one person will shine a bit brighter than others. We shouldn't take this for granted.

However, on this special day, I honor all my colleagues who have been nominated because of their engagement with the community.

Let me be specific. No workforce can be productive without unity, without teamwork, and without strong colleagues. Furthermore, all efforts to achieve a common goal for the community would be wasted without the help of others on the team. It takes only one key person to respect, acknowledge, and recognize all the units; then this can trickle down to the other great individuals.

Speaking of great individuals, those in the frontline unit, part of the emergency unit, saw everything through. Making themselves available mornings, afternoons, evenings, and weekends, they strive to make a difference. This specialty team diagnoses problems and brings about resolutions. They are the decision-makers at the front end of the operation, so they have first contact with the community.

Also, the investigative team is made up of people who are of the same caliber as 007, a team of highly trained individuals chosen explicitly for their ability to extract and analyze all the information critical to the intended outcome and to assist in addressing any legal or political issue. This unit, which is at the forefront, gives an accurate depiction of each situation and sees each to its final resolution.

Furthermore, let us acknowledge a third unit, which is critical to representing the organization and refereeing when appropriate. his team of colleagues is objective in presenting facts, whether related to a new matter or to one that has already been litigated. During each of the three phases, the teams are provided with the critical points. They represent their organization, no matter the decisions they make in the end. This team is better known as the Justice League.

There is also the seasoned team of bold individuals who perform their duties selflessly to protect the community. These fine-tuned teams are known for their strength and teamwork. They would be better known as our operation field soldiers.

Finally, not to be forgotten is the support team, better known as the foundation, which supports all the other units. These people are the mortar holding everything together, working diligently from beginning to end.

Also not to be forgotten are our retirees, along with our fallen comrades. Members who have made the transition will be remembered for their dedication to the organization and to the community. Their memory will always be honored.

Whether community protectors or support staff, we all pride ourselves in working together toward one goal, namely, to serve and protect our community.

So, I decided that to nominate only one person and to forget about the efforts of the whole team would be inappropriate. I opted not to fight the battle and face the consequences tomorrow. So, I moved on and made a better decision by nominating all the teams as one entity.

One is the highest number, and the number four, metaphysically speaking, is the foundation of all matter. In numerology, 1 + 2 + 3 + 4 = 10, breaking down one-to-one consciousness by taking root in one entity. We seek to inner-stand, overstand, and understand the thought pattern that grows the many cosmic roots that branch into many units that equal the one, you and me.

Putting all jokes aside for the moment, I pay tribute to all my colleagues. I first acknowledge the head person who has shown her strength in managing all teams and directing them to stay on the right path, fulfilling their duties and drafting regulations and policies.

Although the head person meets challenges when working with both staff and clients, she strives for excellence. From our managers, I have learned that they enjoy getting up and reporting to work to face the challenge of another day. I have also learned that our managers enjoy our people and love what our organization represents.

I took a moment to speak with many of my colleagues, asking their thoughts about work, unity, and a good old-fashioned love for the job. I was taken aback by the intricacy of many of their concerns.

Just like that, many concerns came to the surface. Some shared that the work was overwhelming. Some shared that the workflow was inadequate and that the job was stressful, exhausting, anxiety-producing, confusing, disappointing, challenging, and surprising, with some saying they were unappreciated and others declining to make a comment. Most, however, expressed their love for the job, their commitment and dedication, their optimism, the fact that they enjoyed receiving good feedback, and the fact that they are supportive of everyone here, but most all they were just being who they are: unique people.

I acknowledge that people will always have differences. Still, as we continue to support our colleagues, our clients, and the community at large, we must never lose sight of the fact that this exceptional group of individuals, our colleagues, could only be together at this particular place and at this particular in time. Remember, we agreed when we signed the contract to come together as one entity, one team, serving collectively with a commitment to valuing teamwork and to making a difference. Let it be known that every day we strive to make a difference in the lives of others.

In the end—and this is long overdue—we honor and give thanks to all the teams, while knowing that we all are the life force of this organization. I tip my hat to you.

Let it be spoken, and let it be heard, that we stand together as one.

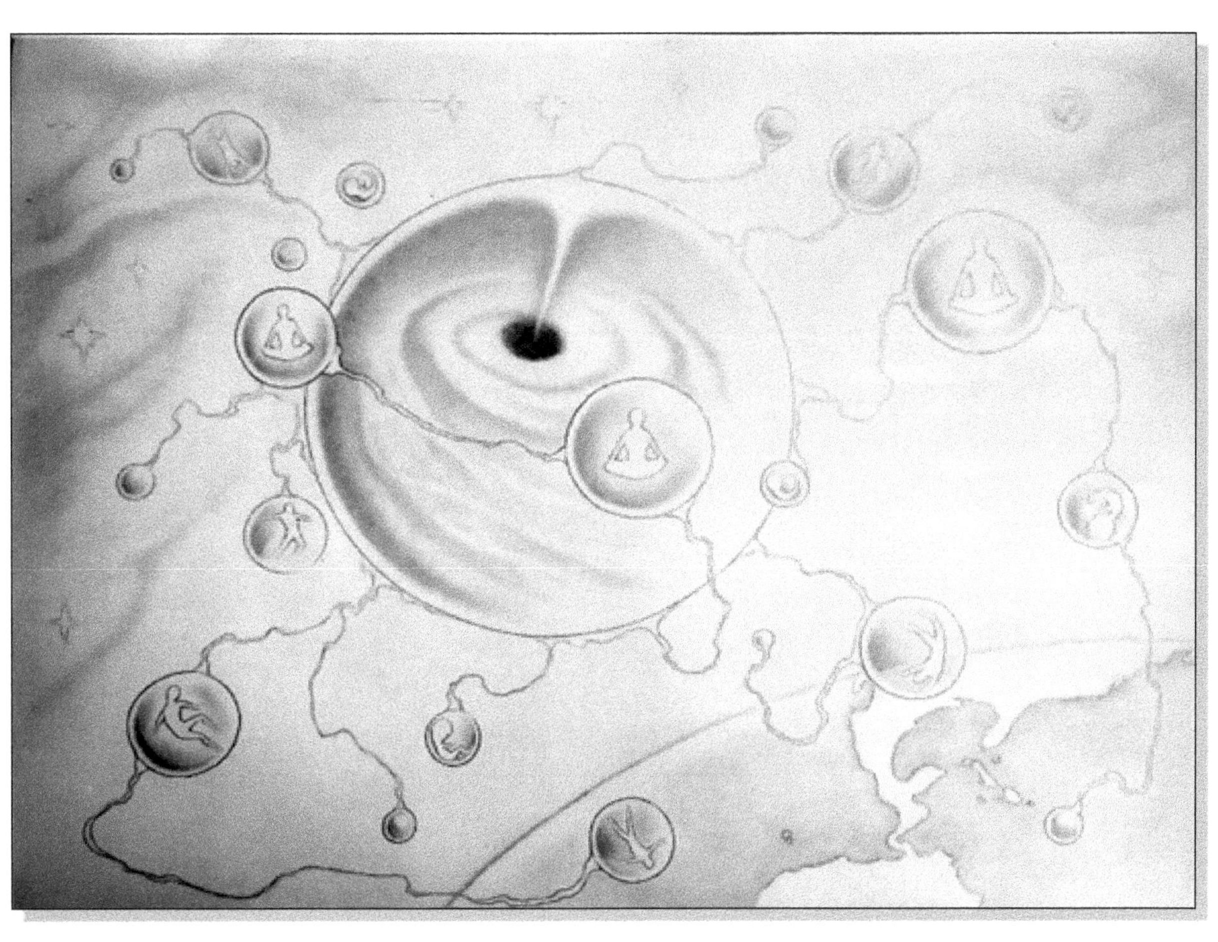

RIGHTS THROUGH ILLUSION

Who gave management the right to separate themselves from the veteran employees and disrespect them, creating a gray area of doubt in the minds of all other colleagues?

Management has recklessly put themselves in the driver's seat, creating turbulence within the minds of experienced veterans and new hires, all the while alienating themselves from veterans and isolating themselves, creating discontent among the veteran workers.

At the root of things, management labels themselves as leaders, but this ship will sink from discontentment.

Management strives to break down the minds of veterans who serve more effectively because of their experience.

This game that plays one side against the other cancels out the efforts and commitment of the workers across the entire organization.

Ultimately, it is these veteran workers and new hires who make the team effective.

XII
XI
I
II
III
IV

TO MY SWEET, DARLING LIFE PARTNER

I write this message to my love.
I give thanks to him for I can only give back,
thanks to our promise of commitment in support of
each other.

I give thanks for your allowing our dream to be
achieved and, with the highest form of commitment,
for your loving me and being loved by me.

Every morning I am honored to arise to
the touch of your body, the smell of your breath,
the sound of your voice, and the flicker of your
eyes as they move and sparkle. I will always long
for these precious moments.

I can only give thanks each day when rising from
sleep that this has manifested into my reality,
allowing my mind to transmit with clarity that
every day I make a conscious commitment to
stay connected to you.

It is important for me to know, and to make it known to you, that I stay as
your wife, a true friend, and that without you—
well, you know the rest.

It is true—always a truth held close
and deep within—that I am
tough, but in reality, I am not as tough as I seem.
I am a gentle soul who only wishes to remain
connected to your soul.

Within me, there is what once was a little child,
now a woman, who inner-stands, overstands,
and understands what a man is to his woman.

I live this life having chosen you to join me on my journey,
knowing that I am safe with you.

I live each day to hold you and to caress every
inch of you, always having the freedom
to reach out and touch your body.
Sometimes I reach out and touch your
spirit.

I live each day honoring your presence,
thus living each day to continue
this journey with you.

I am thinking, as I have thought before,
that we should allow the flow of our ether to do what it does
best, giving thanks to our ancestors, then praising
the higher realm of consciousness that connected you to me
before time began.

What remains of our
fruitful time together, our experiences together, and
all the lessons just waiting for us to learn them together is precious.

I hope it is clear in your mind that these words were written solely for you. This will
be—and I will engrave it onto the vast cosmos—and will remain the glorious time I get
to spend here with you.

Loving my sweet darling is one of my greatest missions.
I rise each morning still loving you,
appreciating all of who you are,
welcoming all the lessons I've learned from you,
breathing with you,
and committing to doing the work needed
to grow this relationship,
to honor you, and to let time do what time does, while it
continues to create for us.

I commit to showing my gratitude while continuing to love the essence of your spirit.

My sweet darling Victor, I am missing you already.

Real talk, my love—just being real with you.

ATTENTION-DRIVEN

I was thinking about being attention-driven.

Is it society that causes an to be individual ego-driven? Do these egos belong to those who are familiar to us or to those who are acquaintances? The people with large egos are similar to the people we see on television. The people who often get behind the wheel to put themselves in the spotlight are mostly individuals with ego problems.

You could say that these individuals lack any form of compassion and have had no nurturing or were somehow denied these things by their parents. heir lack of discipline has made them delusional, so they see a mirror image of themselves, a distorted view of reality.

It came to mind while I was sitting in a quiet space that attention-driven people are highly motivated and intoxicating, having egotistical tendencies.

T hey never stop to quieten their spirits. Not even for one moment do they pause to consider why they do the things they do. Instead, they try to get the attention of those around them.

hey never stop to ask "What if?" or take a moment to breathe or to analyze any aspect of their lives. You see, they are likely too busy working in overdrive to get attention, substituting their drug of choice to fuel them for their next unrehearsed stage performance, which in turn fuels their attention-driven disorder.

I have taken notice of a few of these attention-driven personalities, and I've come to realize that they suddenly appear in front of you, arising as if from nowhere to perform their heroic acts. These unsettling aggressive personalities assert their power to get attention. As a victim, your space is unwillingly invaded while this vampire sucks up your time.

Of course, a person may say that such an individual was merely minding her own business, just strolling along and moving about in whatever direction, when up from nowhere popped an attention-driven individual to distract her attention.

Try to remember the last one-on-one conversation you had with someone, or go back to a time when you were part of a group conversation, a business meeting, a party, or a family gathering.

Did it dawn on you that an attention-driven person managed to take center stage in every conversation and at every event? Did you think that this person was not being treated for attention-driven disorder, leaving it as a force to be reckoned with?

Some might say that all of us want attention. It is reasonable to say that most of us would like to be recognized for a job well done or commended for our high level of artistry or merely for loving our loved ones. But this should not be likened to an attention-driven person's strong desire to be acknowledged.

Attention-driven disorder is a phrase I coined. I may need to do some scientific research to come up with a precise description of those who are attention-driven and to imagine a coping method to address this condition so that we may have a better understanding of those who have attention-driven personalities.

As I quietly looked outward, reflecting on my place in time and in space, it came to my mind that these attention hoarders are also known as the life of the party. They are the talkative ones who speak without any substance to their words.

Those who seek attention are people who let it be known that they know how to do things better than others. Or they may say, "You think you know everything, but you can't save the world." Or they may claim that only their deeds matter.

How do we make sense of the things that we face in day-to-day life? How do we pay less attention to the things we regularly pay attention to, such as certain forms of entertainment?

Why do we lack the power within ourselves to notice the things that prevent our growth, thereby giving power to something that holds no value?

No, we cannot escape these unwelcome conditions that regularly feed off our energy. Still, we should remember that they are around us, coming at us from all angles.

Attention-driven people intentionally, but sometimes unknowingly, take center stage to deliver yet another empty performance.

I decided that I would begin to reduce the amount of attention I pay to those who seek to place themselves within my field of vision and to stay focused on where I am going, staying in my own lane.

MY DIARY AND JOURNAL

My diary and my journal help me keep a day-by-day record of what matters most, becoming a compilation of memories and a pathway to my soul. My log and my journal help to keep me grounded, help me escape from yesterday, and propel me into tomorrow.

As I write in my diary and journal, I think about visions, hopes, and temporary escape. My writing helps to quiet my spirit, helping me understand myself as it keeps me abreast of my plans, the things that I see, and the things that I choose not to share.

I have no immediate need to share my thoughts, as writing in my journal leads to a doorway that opens onto a world of experience and knowledge that is kept private, perhaps to remember at some later time.

Writing in my journal helps me to gain focus. The journal serves as a vehicle and helps me to keep building my path to the future.

Writing in an diary, some say, is old school, but I am here to tell you that writing is an art, something to be developed, a skill that allows smaller thoughts to grow into bigger dreams that become reality. It fosters ideas that help to expand my vision day by day.

Writing in my diary/journal helps me to define myself, yet it also helps me to maintain a balance with the things that matter most.

FAMILY FRIENDSHIP TREE

Remember the times when your grandparents and parents would have longtime friends of theirs come visit? As a child, you often accepted these people as family, calling them uncles, aunts, and cousins.

It was not until you grew up that you learned that these uncles, aunts, and cousins were not your biological family members.

You remember these individuals as usually being more dedicated to visiting the family regularly, being at most family functions, and always being a part of your life. There was never a time when you thought of them as not being family.

It was not until one day, after you were all grown up, that you asked the question to parents or grandparents, "Whatever happened to So-and-So?" You were surprised once your family informed you that these people were never your biological family; in fact, they were only longtime family friends.

Has it ever happened that one of your family friends knew more about the history of your family than those you considered to be biological family members?

Sometimes a family friend is the go-to person when you are seeking information. You find yourself appreciating this person's commitment to your family and its values.

In yesteryears, families and friends of the family were considered to have close connections, so close that they never measured each other's closeness by bloodline.

In life, we sometimes think of our dearest friends as being just like family, so we accept them, sometimes more than we do family, without needing a blood test. This adage applies: "You can't choose your family, but you can choose your friends."

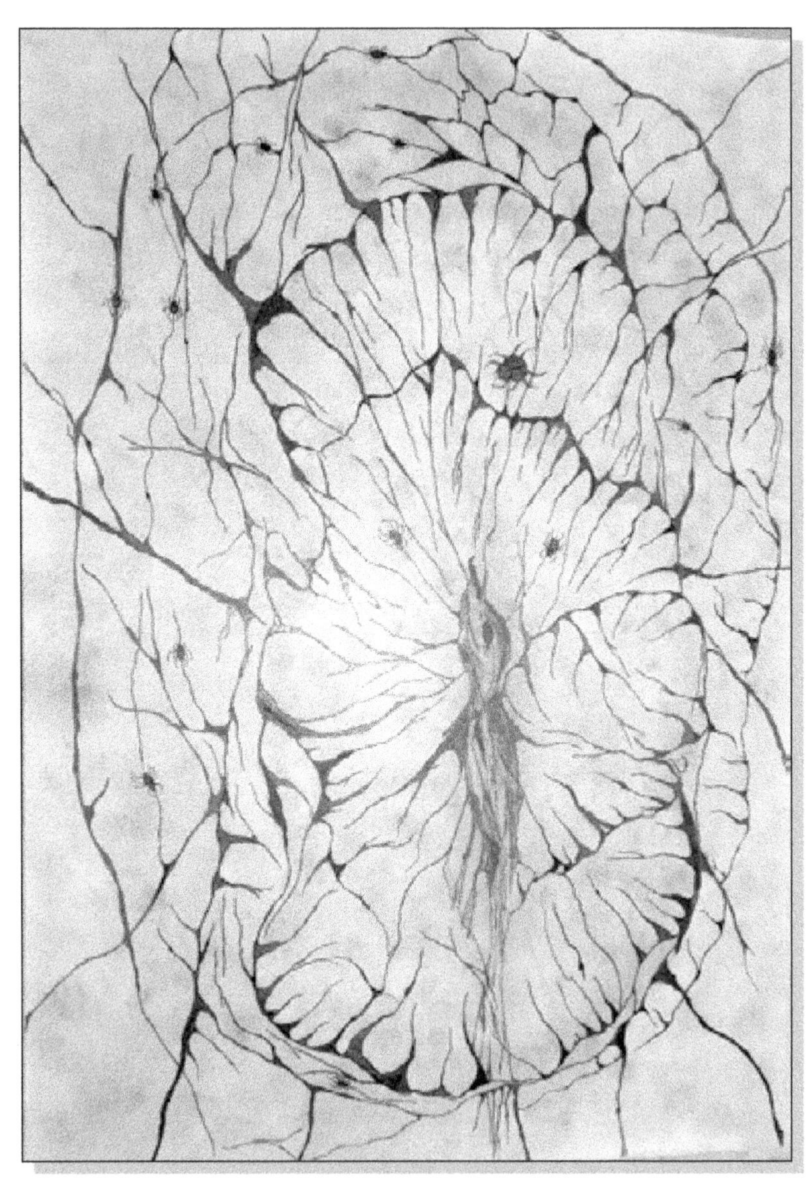

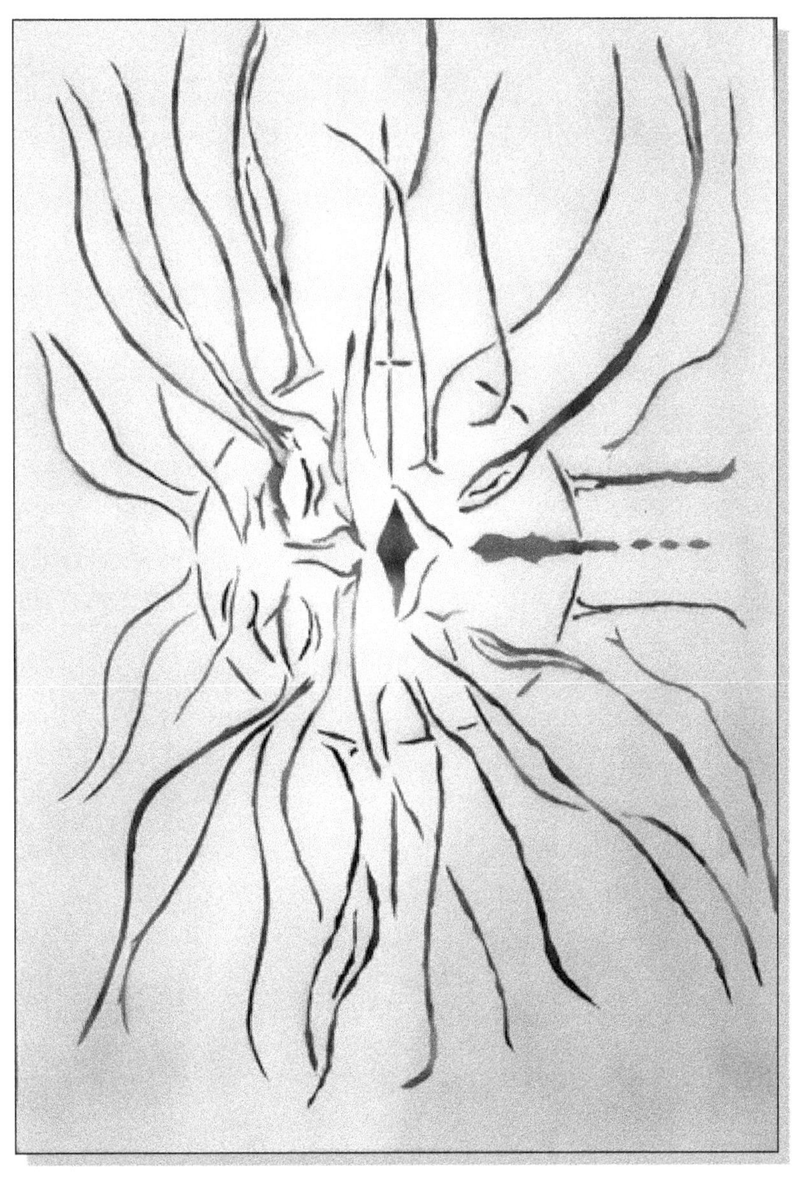

MY CHILDHOOD FRIENDSHIP TREE

I will always remember my childhood friends, whom I hold dear. I will never forget the times that we shared, the playtimes we spent together, or the lessons we learned and later shared.

My childhood was a most exciting time. I still see images from this time that cannot be erased. Throughout my journey of continuous growth, the lessons I have learned have involved endless adventure, joy, and hope.

My childhood began when I first laughed, when I first crawled, when I first stood up, when I first fell, and when I first walked.

My childhood was the beginning of my first lessons, whether staying at home or attending school. At school was where I started to mingle with new classmates who would eventually become my lifelong friends.

At home was where I received my first lessons, beginning with those taught by my parents and friends, only later learning from my schoolteachers.

At the schoolhouse I attended, to make a new friend was to embark upon a new beginning with a chance to socialize and to learn the sorts of lessons that my parents weren't teaching me.

I grew from an adolescent to a teen, during which years my self-esteem and confidence also continued to grow.

I would one day look back at My Childhood Friendship Tree, an album where I once kept mementos from my childhood and wrote down all my dated visions, which inspired me to become the person I am today.

I will continue my journey toward this new beginning by leaning on language and literacy. The friends whom I have loved and communicated with are the people I have met on life's highway. They will continue to inspire me by helping to cultivate my growth. I value the memories I have. They speak of qualities I treasure that help keep me grounded, such as compassion and empathy.

My childhood and teens were a time to embrace life and to build upon my beginnings. From this day forward, I will work on my legacy by remembering those who taught me the life lessons that enabled me to have a voice, starting from my childhood.

As my childhood progressed, it came to shape who I am. Now I am inspired to keep a wealth of memories while building a valuable legacy that I will attach to my childhood friendship tree.

I GIFT YOU

Thinking back on the high points and low points of my life that helped to form my personality and gave birth to my need to be accepted, I sometimes recall the pitfalls I encountered back then.

When I matured and became a teenager, I faced many challenges trying to navigate the ups and downs and to deal with the self-critiques. That is what influenced me to become the person I am.

It's true that self-pity played a role in my development. Feeling sorry for myself brought about many challenges in my growing-up years. Like many younger souls, I tried to learn about the life outside myself. There were times when I thought that I had been defeated and was finished.

Leaving my teenage years behind and approaching my twenties, I experienced the joy of learning about life. I learned by gathering knowledge and then transforming that knowledge into wisdom. This was when I realized that I wouldn't know whether I had made a wise decision until later on.

As I matured, I began to face the fact that I was a little different. When I reached my thirties, my life started to take on a different shape. No more pretending to know what I did not know; I had to put a face on reality.

The reality was that my experiences in life were shaping me as I began thinking more maturely and visualizing and preparing a life plan. The self-pity was now placed on permanent hold. I soon realized that there had never been anyone there to catch me if I fell. Both literally and figuratively, I was faced with taking on the challenges that I had had for a very long time.

Back in my thirties, my life was taking shape more quickly than I had expected. For me, Mama was no longer there, and Daddy had passed on years before. I had no husband or children to support, so I was facing life on my own.

In my forties, I worked to create a different life and stopped allowing past experiences to shape me. I was less bothered by any unwanted negative emotions or by being let down by others, and I could now have a more positive journey by taking full control of the driving force behind my dreams and goals.

In my forties, I have matured to the point of knowing that growing older does not mean an end to setting goals or to wanting more for myself. My thoughts do not have to run rampant, yet my visions do not have to be forgotten and left unpursued. Taking this journey down life's highway, I will continue to appreciate it.

Just like a tree with its roots and many branches, I see that my roots have grown through the ages, and this is a testimony to time: life is unfolding as it should.

I testify to the importance of honoring myself for all that I contribute, helping others and being supportive of them. Also, I know that it is important to be a student of life and to appreciate all of the person I continue to be. I am OK with just being a tree with many roots and branches as I see that such an individual has a purpose in life.

As I drop the anchor on my purpose in life, I still look forward to my continuing growth in the years to come, hoping to make a difference. Ultimately, I look forward to accomplishing my mission to serve humanity.

I ask you, have you given any thought to your purpose in life?

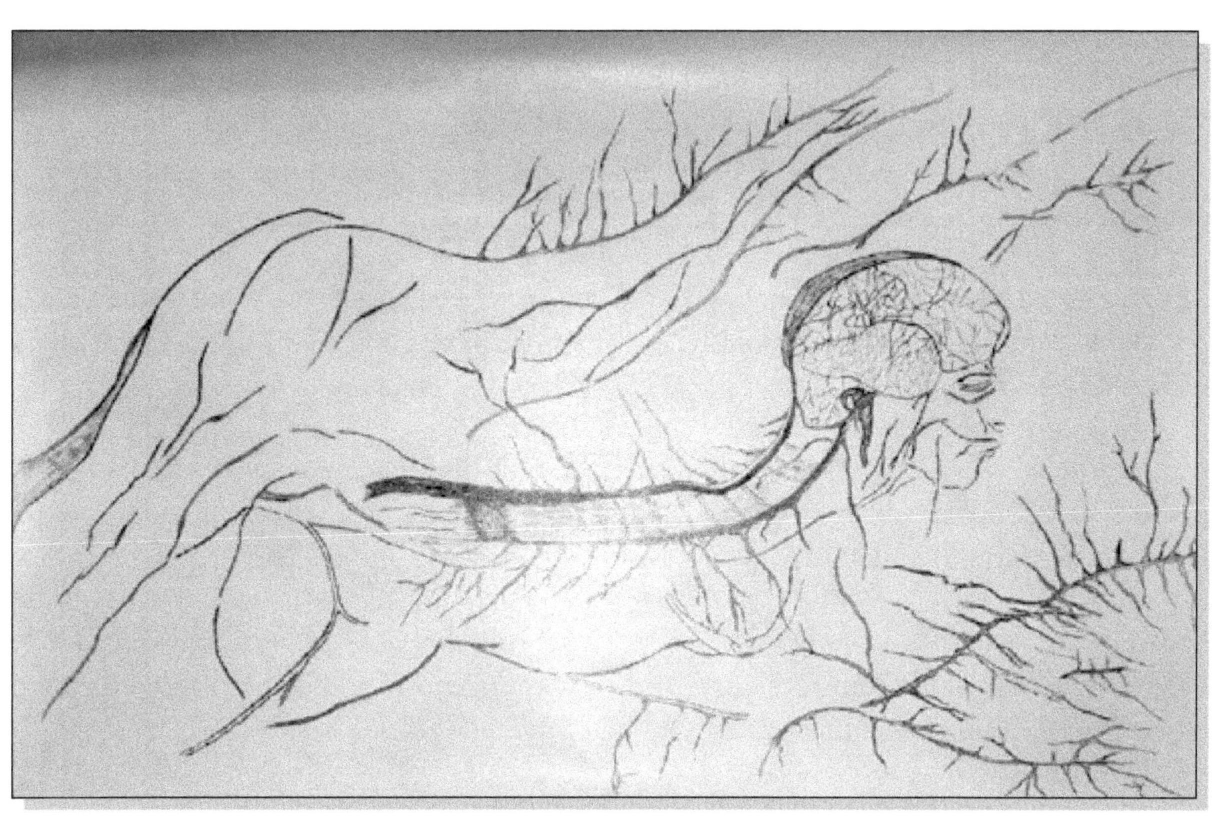

MY CAT NAMED ALIEN

It was cold and rainy one summer day when I learned that my cat named Alien had gone away. No one knows the hurt I suffered. His disappearance temporarily crippled my spirit and distorted my mind.

I often think of the times we shared together, playing hide-and-go-seek, chasing after toys, and jumping high to catch balls of string. I remember Alien often, but I feel the anguish of his not ever going to return. Well, his absence has left a void in my soul. Moreover, although he has been gone for quite some time, his future is still unknown.

I long to spend more time with my pet cat. I will never get him back. It hurts my spirit to know he's gone. I wish that I could have just a little more time with him to soothe my aching heart.

If I could have just a little more time to spend loving him wholeheartedly and looking forward to sharing our old age together. I only want to have a little more time to heal my pain. Maybe it would also help calm the anxiety I feel when dealing with his loss.

If time could stand still, I would tell you that I miss you, Alien, and I wish you were here. If my precious cat would stand still just a little while longer, I would take the opportunity to give him more hugs and kisses.

If I had a magic wand, I would use it to race to hold him tight a little longer. If time were merely a clock that I controlled, then I'd tell my cat named Alien that I am still waiting here for him to come home.

If my time were just a flicker of light, I would shine it on Alien, for he will always be the light that shines close to my heart.

AN ANGEL IN DISGUISE:
MY BEST FRIEND

I arrived home late one night bothered to know that I had left my friend home alone. I knew he was worried about when I would return.

I was concerned about my friend who was at home alone and lonely, as his well-being was always a priority of mine throughout the good times and bad times we shared.

When I think of my friend, I think of his happy spirit, his loyalty, his warm affection, his playfulness, and his willingness to please.

When I think of the moments of joy with my friend, I recall that he was a trusted buddy, a keeper indeed. I appreciate that this is a friend I'll always need.

I am speaking about a true friend of mine, the one I'll always hold dear to my heart. As time has progressed, I have come to count this friend as a family member. He is someone who has earned my loyalty and gained my trust. My friend is an angel in disguise. He is my best friend, a fact I will never deny.

Words can't express the depth of my feelings, but this dear friend of mine is all I've got.

I can't help but share my feelings. This friend keeps me safe and reminds me that love comes in all shapes. He tells me that his passion runs deep within without interruption or wearing a false disguise. He reminds me of how a friend should be with his willingness to show his love, dedication, and devotion.

My friend is there when I need him most, when I need time to talk, when I need to go for a walk, and when I need a shoulder to cry on. He's there to listen. He is a friend indeed, as I describe him to you. When I need someone to hug me, he is there to comfort me and make me feel secure. He is a friend indeed, wiping away my tears and chasing my worries away. He shows me that he is there to comfort me with empathy and affection. He is anxiously willing to give me all his attention and unlimited support.

I am here to tell you that my friend freely gives me the confidence I need when I am faced with any personal dilemma, while reminding me that he has a great deal of faith in me.

When I think of my friend whom I love and trust, I can only say that he will always be my buddy and will remain the pet that I will forever cherish.

MARIO'S DAYS TO GO

He stopped by my office just the other day

just to say hello and pass some time with me.

Pause.

The moment he knocked and came in through the door, I knew he'd tell a story I hadn't heard before,

Like of working in his assigned field and the danger it brings. Often he had shared that those were the good old days.

Mario talked about the unit that he created on his own. He enjoyed protecting the community and ensuring it remained a safe place to live.

Mario talked about his partners in the field and the many things they shared. He expressed his appreciation for them and told me of the experiences they had borne.

Mario spoke of violations and warrants that were handed out, but most of all, he spoke of his colleagues and the way they honored him, which kept him highly driven.

I learned that Mario backed his colleagues and protected them with his life. He was very concerned about their safety because working in this field could cost someone their life.

I learned about the colleagues he had trained in years past as he spoke about their positions within the rank and file.

But mostly he shared his knowledge, the experience he had gained, and the twenty-six years of dedicated service that kept him safe without strife.

When his unit was no longer needed and he had to make a change, he found a new position, one not quite as challenging. Mario, after completing the application and waiting to be accepted, was then assigned to sourcing placement. This new task was not his preference, a job he found himself poorly suited to as he was accustomed to providing hands-on service.

As time went on, while still mastering his skills, Mario saw that his initial displeasure was finally justified. Not a moment passed without a case being ready. Mario made sure that the pending approvals were complete. He was always prepared.

This unit he had created on his own was something remarkable as he continued to work in a pressure zone. But he faced the challenge one day at a time, which is all one can do working with limited time.

We never saw a frown or an expression of distaste on his face, and we never heard him utter a complaint. Mario knew the job had to be done, and he perfected his way of approaching the task so it benefited everyone.

As time went on, he accepted his task and gave out new assignments, much different from the previous ones. Mario now has a new kind of job, having been assigned to a unit supervising clients and tracking files. He has shown no disgruntlement, but he has considered making a new beginning.

We realized when the story had changed.

Mario began counting down to his last days. When the years turned into months, then turned into weeks, then turned into days, he realized he was very close to retirement.

Many others, realizing that the time had come, began counting down too. Mario, we know that you have not changed your mind and decided to stay with us just a little while longer. But it is not retirement that he needed to consider; it was the thought of a final beginning.

With two days to go until his retirement, we should all remember the good times that Mario instigated. We share our love, our blessings, our memories, and most of all our appreciation for Mario, whom we think of with fondness.

And so now we have come to the end. Mario, we appreciate you as our colleague, friend, and partner. As you continue your journey, know that we will remember your dedication, which will not be diminished or fade, as indeed it will continue to bear fruit.

The department, in honoring your twenty-six years of service, will keep in mind the skills that you've developed. May you carry with you the memory of colleagues, present and past, and especially of all fallen comrades, remembering their commitment and honoring them.

We know you talked about the importance of spending time with family and what it means to move on with one's life. So, your plans came as no surprise to us, but we thought we'd make a toast, sing a farewell song, and say a few parting words.

Let us sing for you a song, one that you like and often hear. As we begin to sing the lyrics to this song, remember that you will be missed as we honor you for a job well done.

And now, the toast: Mario, we thank you for your dedication, your commitment to community service, your involvement with group efforts, your sound judgment, your helpful advice, and your endless suggestions. We toast you and honor your positive attitude and the time you contributed. Most of all, we thank you for being who you are.

MY CALENDAR—MY PERSONAL ASSISTANT

My assistant helps me to plan and reminds me of scheduled events, pointing out the specific dates and times.

My assistant helps me stay focused, telling me that I woke up today ready to create another path, one that would propel me in a positive direction, so that my life's journey would have a purpose.

My assistant is unique in every way. It illustrates my day with highlighting colors in a format that allows me to edit, adjust, file, or delete.

It's unique in its setting, reminding me of various appointments, birthdays, anniversaries, seminars, and special celebrations.

My assistant also keeps track of holidays and meetups with friends, and sometimes it reminds me to take a little time for myself.

My assistant is unique, never failing to help me plan for tomorrow. It is a place to keep track of my scheduled events, reminding me that time is the primary thing to keep in mind. It never fails to remind me of the value of time, like looking to the future through a window.

The purpose of my calendar is not only to assist with planning but also to help me organize myself for the future, giving me the versatility to complete multiple tasks and perform many different functions. It allows me to take notes, to send texts, and to write emails by using voice activation. It enables me to plan events, and it reminds me of those events.

With appreciation for the many functions my assistant performs, I want to finally share that it organizes my activities on a daily, weekly, and monthly basis.

LIFE

Life sometimes is only one's perception of it and one's way of reacting to it. At times, we measure our growth by considering the things we have learned through experience. We recall those times when we overcame our emotions and found solutions to our problems.

Sometimes we are unsure of ourselves or of how politics and economics influence our lives. Sometimes, we may try to solve our problems by relying on our emotions rather than applying wisdom or obtaining knowledge through diligent research.

We sometimes fail to apply the right degree of wisdom in developing more positive relationships, whether they be personal relationships, work/business relationships, relationships with our children, or relationships with our friends.

Perhaps we should apply what we have learned from our own experience and from that of others to enrich our own lives. This would help us to understand the mechanics of life and its importance to things both tangible and intangible.

I mentioned that we all have learned life lessons. But as I converse with my higher self and other people, I see that our thoughts and how we apply them when taking action determines how our lives will unfold.

What is the meaning of life? I conclude that we continuously create experiences for ourselves, learning many lessons as we challenge ourselves.

Although we challenge ourselves to develop and grow, we may experience twists of fate.

We challenge ourselves sometimes without being fully conscious of the road we are traveling or whether it will influence our decisions in the end. Some of the roads seem to be endless as we may reflect on those decisions that we made before, not knowing that we were taking a wrong path.

We fail to question ourselves about our choices or to be held accountable for our actions. Sometimes, we opt for the easier path of blaming others.

By chance, when learning about consequences, we may make the necessary adjustments. Then we can use the wisdom we have gained from our experiences to help us avoid unfortunate outcomes.

How original and individual are we, really? Or do we mimic others' words, style, innovations, and ideologies and call this creativity, without taking the time to understand these things? Are we using our analytical skills to gather the information we need to solve our problems?

We sometimes fail to acknowledge the things we have learned, yet we hold onto them as our own. How do we even begin to reach a higher level of wisdom and become more effective and better disciplined without undergoing the experiences that lead to the life lessons imposed on us by high society?

When I think about the word *life*, I wonder about my own journey to enjoy life, being open to understanding the many layers of life's lessons. I find myself being open to growth to gain wisdom for success. As I continue to share my experiences and my concerns, I will try to make each step count by following a more accurate road map.

Life has a plethora of layers and outcomes. However, one thing for sure is that it allows each person to live life the way they want to, because no one else can make the journey for us.

When I think of life, wondering about its purpose and why my spirit exists in this physical body, I conclude that the spirit is the puppeteer of the soul, which the spirit animates.

I would like to share that I am still learning.

NOT AGAIN

When your second marriage has failed and loss is the only return on your investment, just apply God consciousness and disentangle yourself from whatever it is that resulted in the decision to end the marriage you both had committed to.

You should not challenge your partner and ask why he or she committed transgressions without checking to see if you failed to use foresight, which led to the negative outcome.

It's better to gather your wits and realize that although love has been lost, life will continuously provide you with upgraded road maps and with experiences that you can invest yourself in.

Do not try to work out something that should be left alone. You should move on.

Better not to remain with someone who is no longer meant for you than to play the game of wanting to breathe with the person who will not practice deep breathing with you.

I WILL NOT CRY AGAIN

It took a while for me to pull myself together after traveling down a path that I thought was hopeless.

Exactly two months to the day when it first happened, I found myself in a dark space, thinking I had failed. You walked away from something that I thought had mattered: being a husband to me.

Trying to find the strength to deal with this tragedy, I found that my sanity was leaving me.

I challenged myself, trying to find other ways to handle my sorrow. At one point, I decided not even to think about why you had decided to leave me.

Now that I had to face the fact that I was alone, I crumpled, falling to my knees, which only made matters worse. Days passed, but still I could not think clearly. Without the hope of your return, I didn't see the point of going on.

I didn't hear from you for many days, then the days turned into months. I listened, wishing I could remember the sound of your voice.

I began questioning myself and repeatedly asking myself why you had chosen to leave. Having swiftly gone from sharing a life with you to being alone, I felt defeated, having no idea why I would feel that way.

Blindsided and in a state of shock, I could not control my grief. Stricken with it, I could not conjure up the strength to function.

I found myself suddenly sick and riddled with pain, trying to figure out just how I was going to deal with my circumstances.

I failed to stand when what I needed was to get up and walk. I failed again and again, forcing myself to eat, eating only to sustain my life.

I tried to face the image in the mirror but could not bear seeing myself in such a state of misery, as facing myself would only force me to admit that I was in agony.

The only way I could think of to maintain my sanity was to pick up a damn pen and start writing. Now maybe I would start to figure things out.

Writing about my pain, my life, and my marriage brought me temporary solace.

I kept writing down my thoughts and my feelings. Now I am telling my story in a poem, the story that I have been waiting to share with all of humankind. Indeed, I still suffer, existing in a state of constant sorrow.

I admit, it was difficult for me, but as I poured my heart out, writing about this whole mess, this life change, this crossroads, I began to cry, my tears pouring down as if from a rain cloud.

I can't help but wonder, did my soul lose its energy, or did someone try to steal its energy?

I kept questioning my sanity. I kept trying to hold onto what I assumed was nothingness.

Eventually, I had to pull myself together and stand tall, knowing that I was not a victim. And to face the bottomless well of love I had for you and for us, I needed to somehow muster the strength to stand on my own. So, I asked out loud, "Do you hear me?"

It is essential to tell you that I was reaching deep down into the pit of understanding. Indeed, I couldn't reach any deeper into my core, my soul, the place where my energy dwells. Eventually, my spirit talked back to me. I give thanks for having been given the strength to embrace my weakness.

I tried not to question my first thought, which was of exchanging wedding vows with you, as I wasn't the one who had broken those vows. You were. Maybe after walking away from me after sixteen years of marriage and giving me no explanation for it, you understand that you failed to honor your commitment. On this I stand firm.

I will not reach out to you for any explanation. I will not cry again. I found solace within myself, having come to know that it's OK for me to cry out in pain, as that is evidence of the love I had for you and the sorrow I felt because we were no longer a couple. I decided that I would not cry again. I was tired of struggling, looking for reasons for this and reasons for that, asking myself if I'd done something wrong. I decided I would not cry again and that I would never ask if you ever even loved me at all.

I decided not to burden my friends or family with my troubles when really it was my own business.

I will get up, and I will walk again. I will eat to feed my spirit again. And now I'm getting ready to face the image in the mirror again.

Today, I understand that sometimes things happen that we cannot control. So, I dare not ask if love is love. As I move forward, I will continue to travel life's highway, which is continually upgraded with many new lessons to aid us as we walk along this spiritual path.

My vow to you, my husband, is to continue treating you with the utmost respect and to honor your privacy. I strive for good morals, ethics, values, and standards as we continue to grow, both independently and jointly, keeping it real with ourselves and with our spirituality. I accept that our commitment will always be in concert with itself.

It's not much to say, but when we were first introduced, I had no idea where we would end up. I kept an open mind, anticipating many possibilities. So, I say passionately that I have found more meaning and purpose in life since having shared my life with you and loving you.

Even though I had vowed not to, I cried one more time, upon your return home. I shall ask no more questions about the journey we are still on. Now, several years later, our love remains. You asked me for forgiveness, which I granted, and our commitment to one another remains strong.

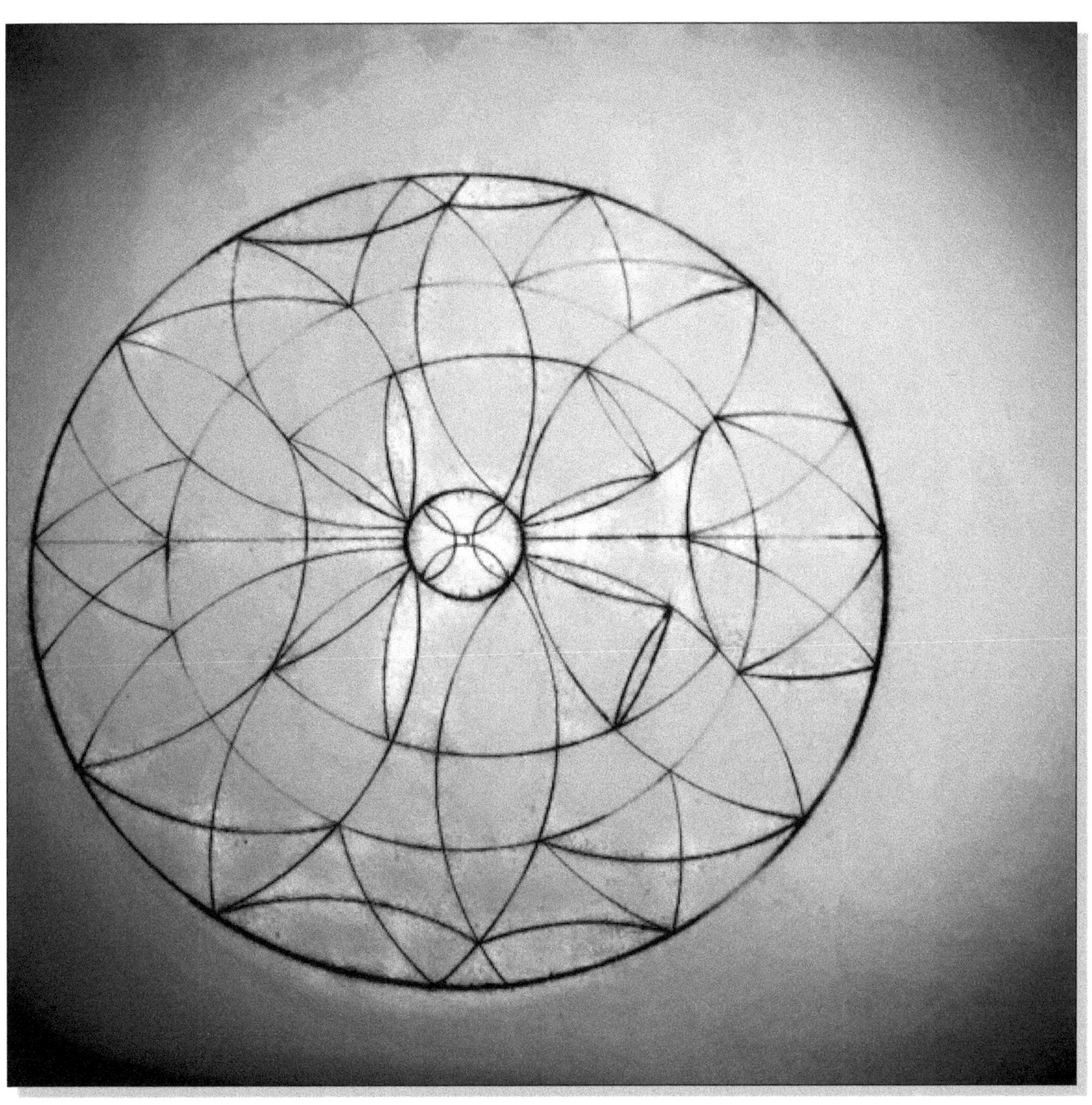

KEEPING WITH THE STROLL

Humans are strolling down a pathway, traveling wherever life's journey takes them.

You could never imagine who or what you may encounter on your journey through life.

You may never know the talent you have without the circumstances to stimulate its development.

You may never learn of the wisdom to be found within yourself, wisdom that could be of benefit others.

You may never know that you can craft knowledge into a positive tool.

You may never realize that lending someone else a hand could help them realize their dreams.

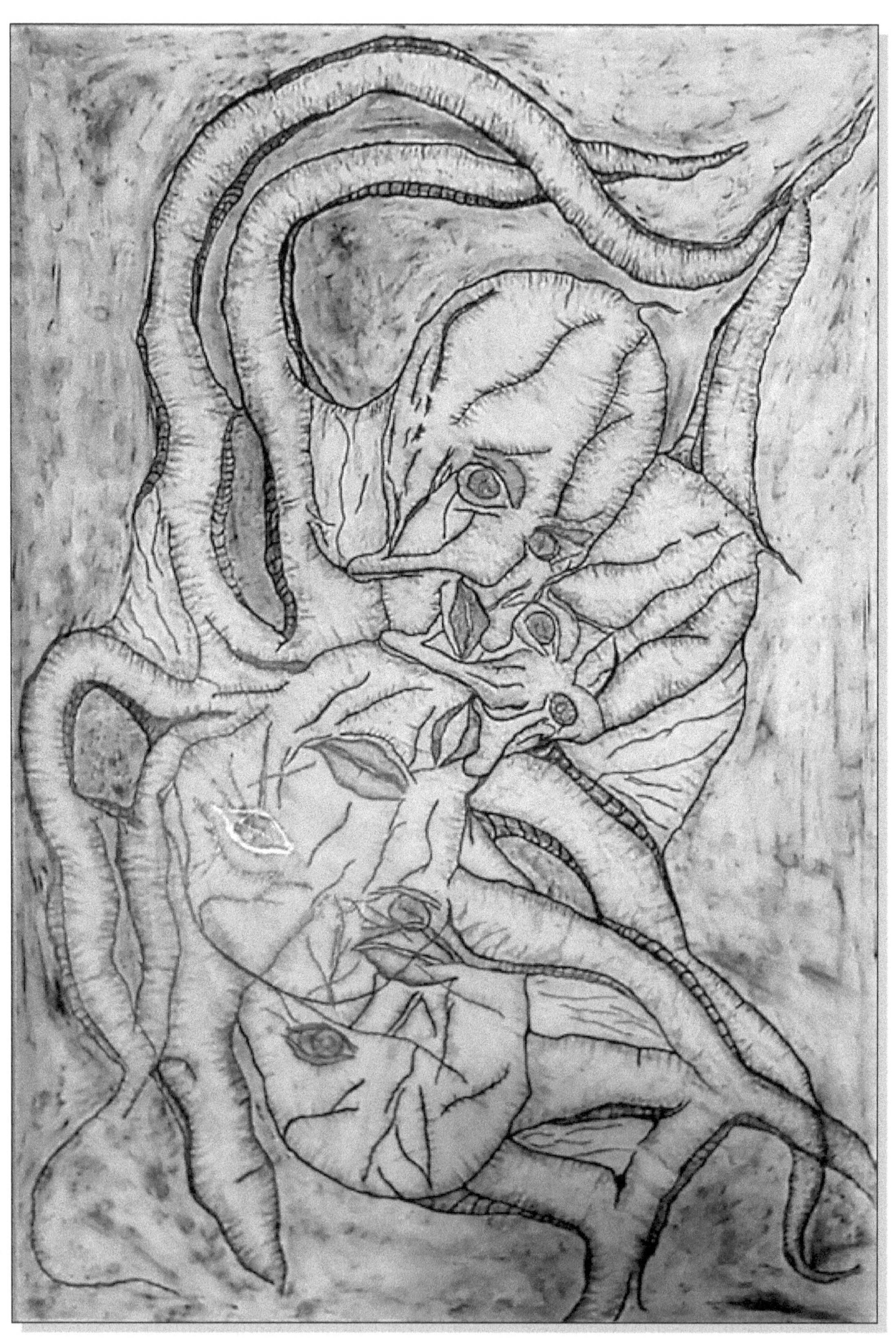

Let Us Not Drown in Our Own Feelings

Your knowledge could beget wisdom, which could be shared with many.

You may never know that your life experiences could help shape how a nation is educated.

If you don't love yourself, you will never know that you are unique.

You may never know that your efforts actually helped build up someone else's confidence, empowering not only that individual but also many other people.

You will never know the power of sharing if you don't ever share.

One act of selfishness closes your hands to receiving.

Pretending to be tolerant and kind is different from believing someone else is beneath you because that person is foolish.

Don't believe that you will get away with your lies forever. You have failed to go within yourself in search of the truth.

Sometimes It Gets Deeper

We speak about the desire to change. Let's touch on these indicators of change:

A smile from you could brighten another person's day.

A friendly touch from you could comfort someone else's heart.

You may never see the footprints of the person who saved your life.

If you don't know the power of thought, then you might never know that you can turn a dream into reality.

Stop running away from yourself. Take the time to discover who you are.

You May Not Know

You may not know that you have value and that you speak words of wisdom to others.

You might not know that some of the things you have done in your life remain useless because you have done them for your own benefit, not for the benefit of others.

You Should Know

Give only as much advice as you are prepared to take.

Yesterday should remind you of what to do today.

No one owns your mind, nor does anyone have the right to control it. But you yourself may keep it in bondage, which is a foolish choice.

We are each made up of ever-evolving energy with its infinite possibilities in terms of shape, form, and type.

A tree will not eat if it has no roots or breathe if it has no leaves, both of which ultimately sustain its life. You, who embody the true essence of life, would not be here today without those who came before you. Those who come after you will continue the circle of life.

Allow any mistakes you make to turn into an opportunity to gain knowledge, experience, and wisdom.

Know that your attitude is affected by what you read, the television shows and the movies you watch, the people you interact with, the activities you engage in, the music you listen to, the environment you live in, and the food you eat.

You are the sole product of your past, present, and future.

With time being an unknown, you are the creator of your own past, present, and future.

Remember

Your heart will express love if you develop awareness.

The words you speak could uplift another.

You could use your hands to perform CPR and restore a person's heartbeat, saving their life.

Sharing a laugh with someone else brings them joy and reignites their spirit.

God is the universal consciousness within you that has created wonderful things to share with the masses.

A person, being universal consciousness, should continue to manifest love, which will conquer all.

As You Go along Life's Journey, Do Not Forget

You might never find out that you have the ability to bring joy and make a difference in someone else's life.

You may never know the support that is available to you. If only you were open to receiving it.

You may never know that you possess enough strength to save another person.

You might never know that the words of kindness you speak to someone else may carry them for the distance.

You may never know how the love you give to another makes a difference in their life.

You may never know that your willful ignorance, not wanting to know the truth, comes at a steep cost.

Resurfacing into Wellness

It is OK to share a secret if it will save someone else's life.

You may not know that investing in yourself increases your value.

Work to Make a Difference

You might not know that if you cause the death of another, you will forever be in arrears of your debt.

Stress on your heart will lower your quality of life.

If you are quick to judge, judgment of you will be swift.

You may not know that to judge a person because of their skin color, creed, religion, education level, social status, and/or wealth is to take a step backward. You too will be judged for your lack of humanity, your lack of humility, and your disregard for others.

Your backward thinking to justify your bad behavior will not prevent you from suffering the consequences.

You may not realize that a spell has been cast upon you. You continue to think that you are free in this world over which you have no control.

You Must Know That ...

If you try to ruin another person's opportunity, then you may find that your own opportunities are limited.

Every time you act out of jealousy, you are fighting with yourself for failing to develop your own greatness.

Every time you encounter a difficulty, quiet your mind, as a quiet mind thinks up better solutions.

Every time you say that you know already, without allowing the other person to finish what they're saying, you are just showing your ignorance.

Every time you use evil to trick another person, the forces of creation will act against you.

What if You Knew?

Whenever a person reveals their true self, don't make excuses for what they've said or how they've acted.

If a person to whom you are attracted is not attracted to you, do not consider it as rejection, but as a message that you should move on.

Know that life is like a shuffled deck of cards, and the hand you are dealt is yours to play to the best of your ability.

If you rob someone else of their love, faith, property, or life, then it will have an adverse effect on you. You will repay the debt many times over.

Know that harboring negative energy against another means that harm will likely come upon you.

When you pump a person up and then turn around and attempt to destroy their confidence, you will be outed as a trickster.

When you attempt to sabotage someone else, your lies will be exposed.

When you misconstrue another's words and twist them to your own purposes, know that others will see your attempt to destroy something good. Justice for your actions will not be in your favor.

When Enough Is Enough

Stop fighting with yourself, thinking that you are unworthy, and cease allowing others to define you.

Stop promoting self-hatred from a poor mindset with low self-esteem.

Stop badgering yourself with thoughts of not being good enough when you have not asked the question "Good enough for whom?"

Stop letting others shape your reality just because you have neglected to create your own.

Never envision an end to your life, as it could block the thoughts needed to create a better you.

Stop second-guessing the image in the mirror, or you might give excuses for not being your authentic self.

Stop believing information other people give you as gospel truth. Dig deeper, doing your own research, to confirm what you hear.

Stop thinking negatively about things you haven't yet learned about. Know that harnessing some energy could be beneficial to you.

Stop thinking that you have solved a problem you have created and self-diagnosed, thinking that killing a person outweighs having a conversation.

A Time to Reconsider

Stop allowing others to inject you with unknown solutions that may compromise your life, such as IV drugs; food that is touted as superior but that may otherwise compromise your health; and toxic water that may have been made toxic by people with an agenda, and stop refusing to follow the money trails to determine who it is that seeks to earn a profit from your self-destruction.

Stop blaming another for your wrongdoings when you are the architect of those wrongdoings, with the truth now waiting to be visited upon you.

If someone has been unfaithful to a commitment they made to you, blindsiding you, know that this is the universe's way of filtering out waste from your life.

Stop discrediting other people and the great things they create just because you want to be at the center of attention, when you haven't bothered to produce anything yourself.

Stop the bloodshed in other lands. In escaping the bloodshed, you must return to your own nation to regain your freedom.

Stop denying another the opportunity to shine brilliantly when you have not bothered to polish your own abilities.

Stop denying that someone else's merits got you promoted, and stop accusing people of not using you as a prop to keep others under control.

Stop welcoming others as messengers to your realm without investigating their merits. Beware of manipulators who wish to harm you and distort your mind. Also be mindful of any collaborators who arrive with smiling faces without asking who sent them in the first place.

I Believe I've Got It

Stop making excuses for failing to remove anything toxic from your life. This one life is all you have.

You could be a better person if only you would quieten your inner self and allow life to create life.

Do not give others the power to either validate or invalidate you. Gain courage by refusing to let others determine if your life matters because of your skin color, social class, and so forth.

Rid your soul of any negative energy by saying out loud: "I am done with any negativity that may cause harm to another or bring about any affliction upon me; I am done with allowing others to control me; I do not consent to any theft of my soul's energy; I release myself from any contracts that hold me in bondage."

SHARING MY THOUGHTS

As I begin to search my soul, I find
myself drifting in and out of thoughts
about you.

I yearn to hear your
perfumy voice as it gently
whispers sweet words into my ear.

Like getting butterflies, it makes me quiver.
And if that isn't enough, I find myself
having sleepless nights, awake and trying to
find answers to things that
will soon come to pass.

It's not enough to say that I long for these
precious moments, seeing them as precious
stones, as I have waited all my life
to meet you.

It's not enough to know that the universal
creation has delivered—no, has placed
before me—a positive atom that will continue
as part of my life journey.

These atoms—protons,
electrons, and neutrons—can surely form pure
energy from your very essence.

Silly, huh, that I am behaving like a
schoolgirl who wants to dance to the first song,
but in essence, I know that the music never
stops playing, nor have I stopped hoping

or dreaming of that special schoolboy,
now grown into a man, I would like to dance with.

As we continue to grow and learn about
each other, this time will pass, and I will graduate
from behaving like a silly schoolgirl to behave like
the woman you have been searching for.

And if that woman be I, and if that
man, well, be you, then may
our bond be cemented.

Kinda like two atoms that once
danced together and now make sweet
music together, but

Just like music, when the words
to express the thoughts are unclear,
the music—well,
the music never fails you.

January 17, 1999

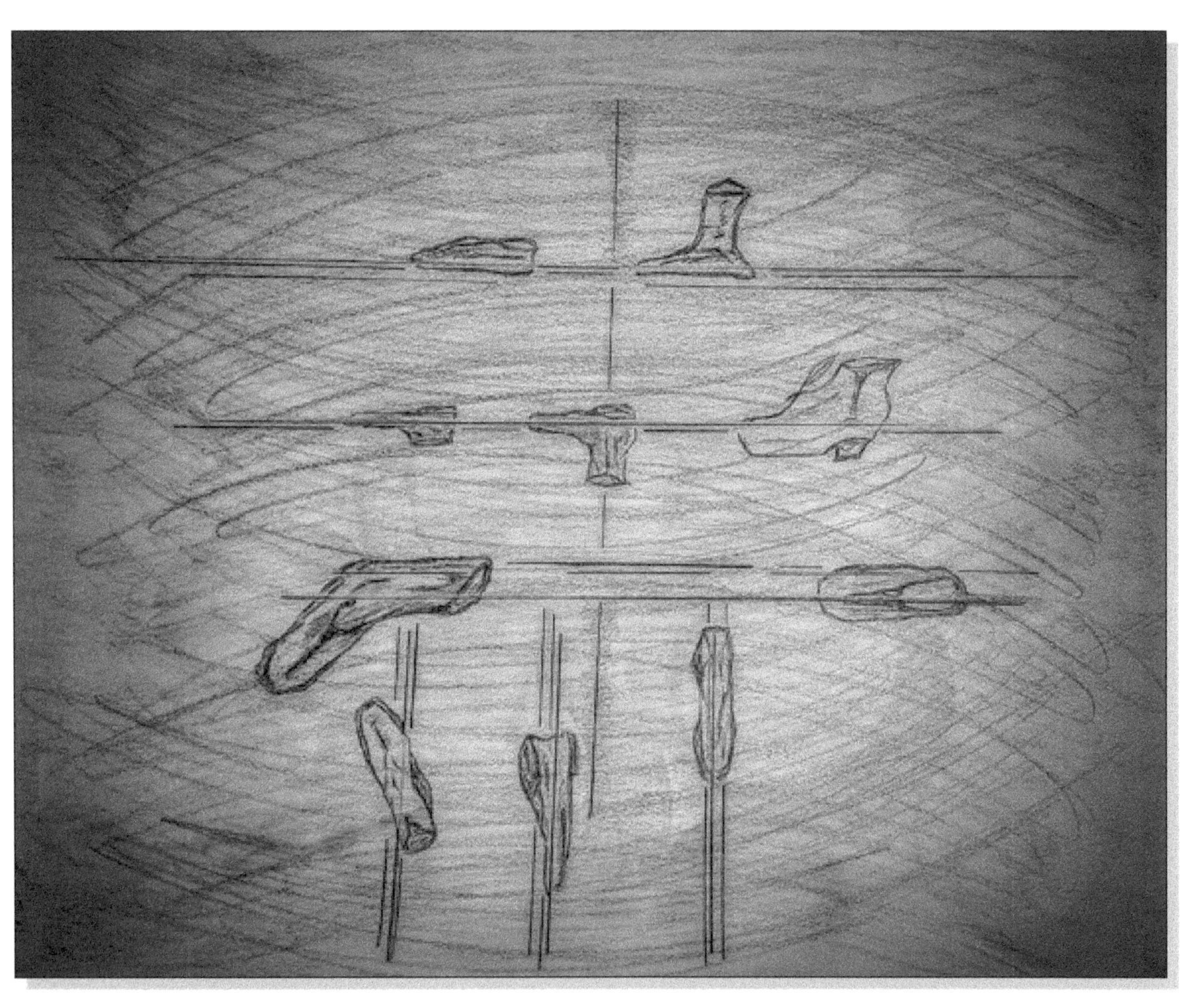

EVERY TIME I LEARN

Every time I learn of your difficult situation, I can only express my empathy.

I feel your pain; I understand your state of agony;

I have learned of your false imprisonment; and I give you my sympathy for your defeat and your suffering.

I am angered by your wrongful death. I feel that I carry the world on my shoulders every time I learn of another senseless loss.

Sometimes I need to pause for a moment before taking the next few steps to rationalize the burden of sorrow that human beings carry.

Your pain has become engulfed within my energy. I just need a moment to sit down and breathe.

THE KILLING WILL END

You're killing me while I am standing, killing me while I'm sleeping, then trying to kill me when I'm fleeing.

You killed me while I was playing outside my home. You shot me while I was dining with friends.

You made a strategic decision to kill me while I was attending church services; you killed me while I was attending school. And the killing happened again when I was on vacation. You killed me when I was taking flight.

You decided to kill me while I was jogging, swimming, hunting, romancing, and partying.

Others witnessed you killing me when you found me in a love entanglement. You killed me out of jealousy, killing me in love and war.

You shot me while hiding behind false accusations. Then you strangled me to death, killing me while talking about civil rights; killing me because of my human rights; killing me when I was pulled over by a traffic police officer; then killing me on the streets.

History has proven that one thing is certain: the killing of me will not end.

But there will be a reaction to these killings, and unfortunately for you, there will be a different end.

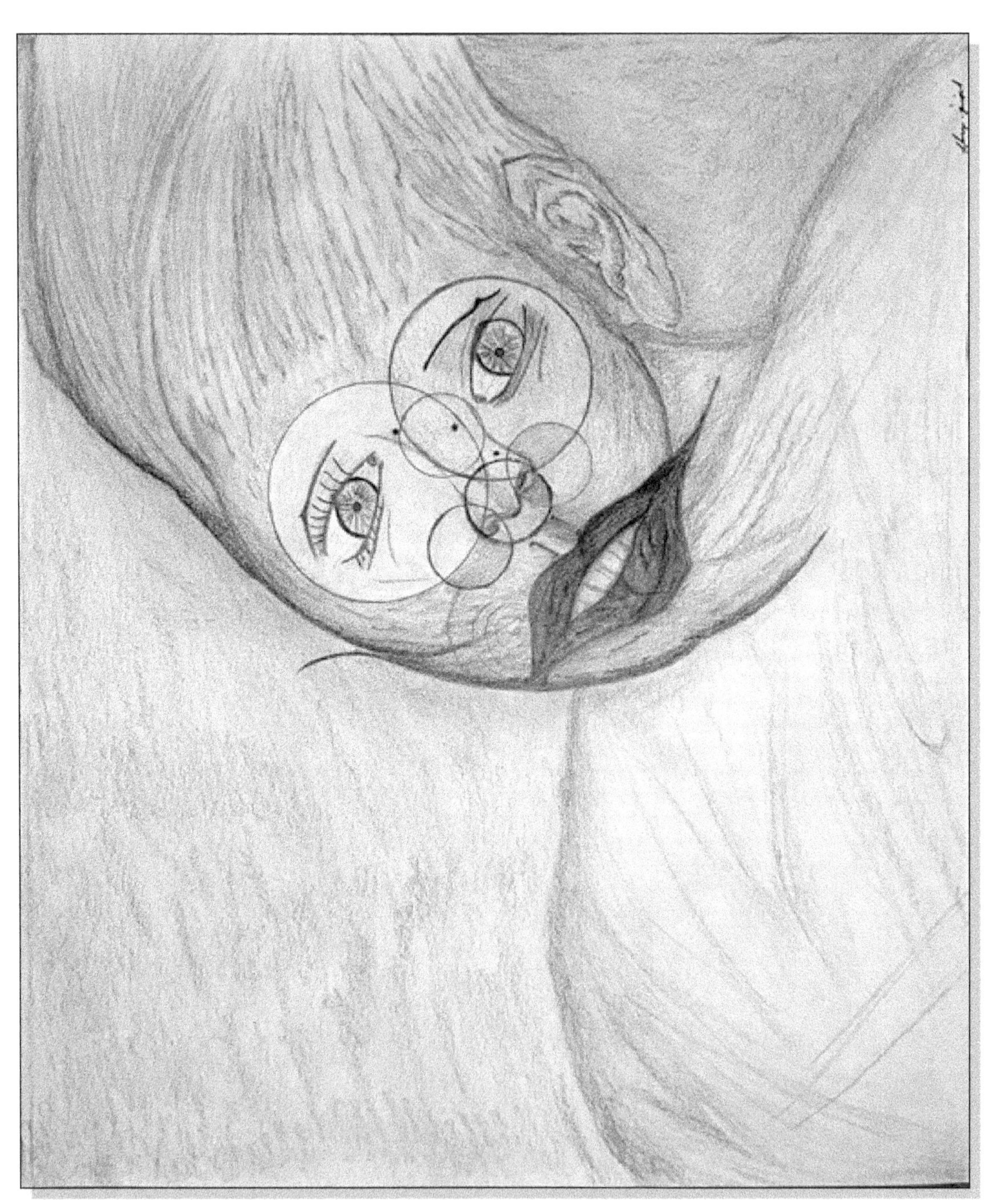

V-O-I-C-E

Do you hear me?

Do you see me?

I exist within myself, not outside myself.

My mind is quiet, only listening, speaking no further, for I am learning.

I did something that most would see as unforgivable, leaving others quiet, unable to speak.

There was darkness left inside of me, and it tore me apart to know that I did not accept the person I carried within me. I was bothered by not wanting to face this person in the mirror, as I believed that others had placed a spotlight of shame on my stage.

As I remember that unattached feeling of emptiness caused me to fall silent with blame.

Who are you, really?

What's eating at your soul?

Who told you that you do not matter?

Have you ever told yourself that you matter to yourself and that you are able to love yourself?

Why wait for others to tell you that you matter?

If you did not matter to someone yesterday, will you matter to them today?

Yes, I blamed myself for trapping myself in a place where I felt lonely with nowhere to stand, nowhere to go.

No one knew the suffering or the pain that I endured. I was facing my fear alone while looking into the mirror. Yes, I called it fear.

Sometimes I laugh in order to hide my sadness, and I engage in conversation with others to pretend that I am not lonely. Other times, I find myself trying to make peace with myself, making my way to a place where I sometimes hide.

I coined the phrase *voice double Dutch* after having my voice stampeded over and being unheard when socializing with others and wanting to tell my story.

It's true that I found myself speechless and unacknowledged when I wanted to be listened to. It became a battle of voice double Dutch. I was left struggling to jump into conversations to voice my opinions.

Do you want to hear me? Do you want to see me?

Sometimes when I try to speak and share my opinions, I feel fear, which I keep inside, with no one taking the time to hear me and with no one caring to know who I am. So, I stand here in front of the mirror once again, practicing saying the things that I would like to share, still knowing that these things matter only to me.

Once, when I tried to interject by speaking out loud, I began to pull back. When I swore, I heard the voices of others, who were sniggering at me. As I tripped over my words, I suddenly became nervous about the things that I wanted to share.

It took a little time for me to realize that these things mattered to no one else but me.

Today, I am free as I stand tall on my square, knowing that I exist within myself and that I live outside myself. I take this stand so that I may finally come to terms with myself, finally realizing that what I say does matter. It's OK for me to have an opinion, just as I respect the opinions of others, holding no objections to anyone's exercising of their right to speak their mind.

I did something that most would see as unforgivable, leaving them quiet. Back then, I chose to quieten my voice because I was too weak and too afraid to commit myself. I was afraid to use my voice to speak of my concerns or to give my opinion.

I am stronger now. I have more experience; I have grown to a much higher level of wisdom and can define myself now.

I now realize that what I did was not something unforgivable. I now choose to exercise my right to use my voice.

I can hear myself now, I can see myself now, for I am continually refining my presence. My voice will be heard.

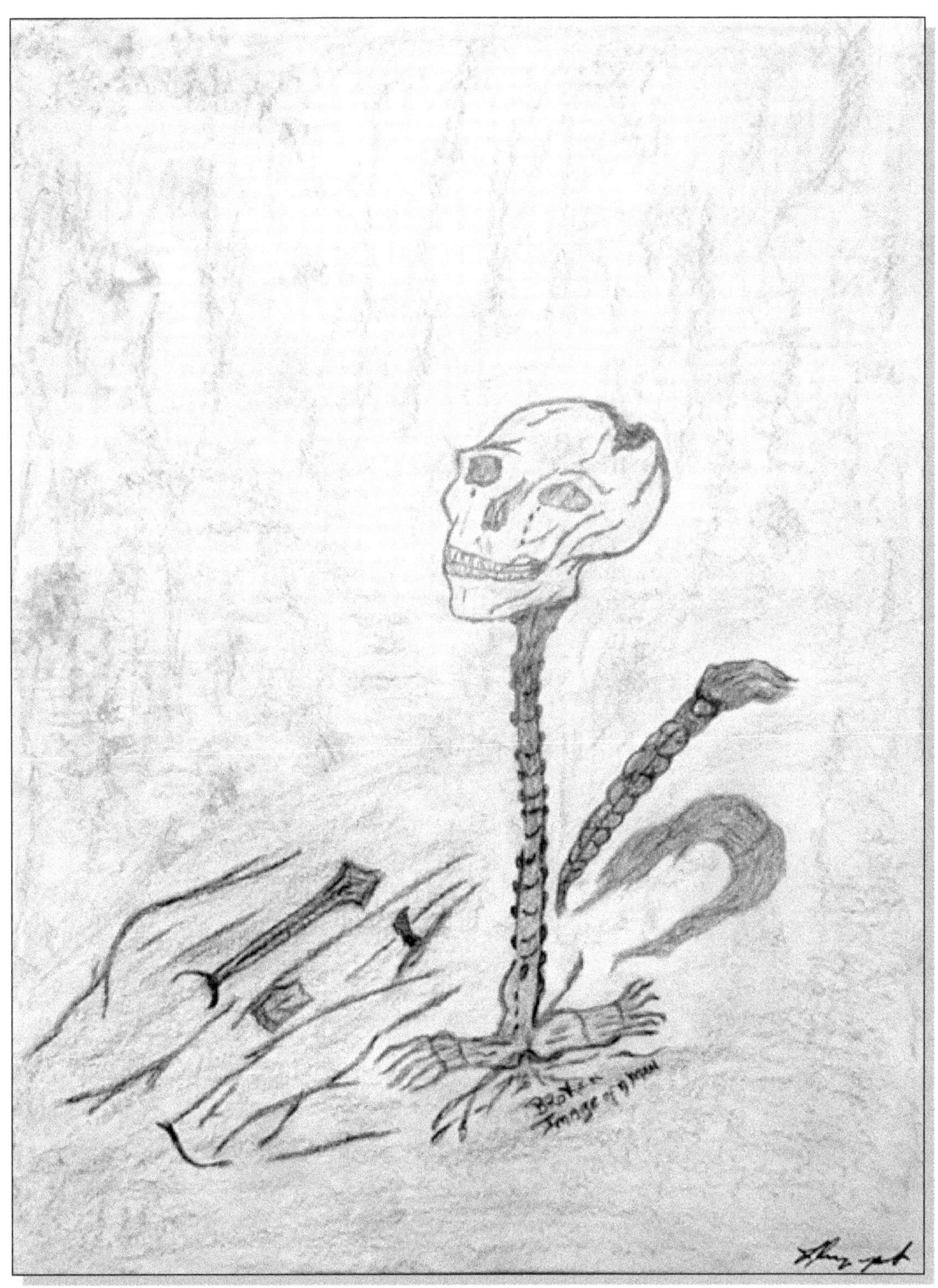

Broken
Image of a man

A SHARED COMMITMENT

To ensure the success and security of the next several generations, I commit to transferring wealth into their hands and passing on the right tools. This wealth and these survival tools will continue to accumulate for generations.

I have made a commitment to stop buying anything extra. Therefore, I am changing my habits and only purchasing the basics, refusing to buy things that I want but don't need.

I am committed to investing in the future by building healthy communities with a strong economic base.

I am taking a final look in the mirror to reevaluate myself and question why I let my selfishness keep me from succeeding and reaching my goal, failing to consider those who preceded me.

I forbid myself from making excuses for my parents' failure to build a future for me.

I intend to move away from the idea of spending everything while I am alive, because I cannot take it with me. On top of that, I would be a failure as a parent if I were to decide not to invest in property assets, where the real wealth is.

I have stopped nagging my children and telling them that they must move out of the house when they come of age, thrusting them out into an unknown world before allowing them to accumulate any wealth.

I have stopped telling the younger ones what they need to do for themselves, saying they should not depend on their elders for advice to enhance their future.

I stopped looking for that which is outside of me to take care of my personal responsibilities, no longer relying on the system or a corporation to solve my problems. Therefore, I support building a future for the generations to come.

I am considering what I can contribute to build a better tomorrow. I am creating the blueprint as we move ahead to lay the foundation for the next century (beginning in the year 2100) in this millennium.

I'M JUST SAYING

If you deny a person the opportunity to advance in your company, then you unknowingly pass the baton of prosperity to a competitor.

Sooner or later, you will learn that you have helped remove any obstacles standing in this person's way and have opened doors, which will help this individual to gain what is needed to move forward, work on his or her strengths, and gain the insight to make the commitment to master his or her craft.

Later you learn that this former employee has created a business that competes with yours on the market, helping to shape society at large.

You will learn from this that misjudging a valuable employee weakens your game on the proverbial chessboard.

TIRELESSLY SEARCHING

All those years of tirelessly looking for God, searching endlessly for something never seen, never touched, never heard, never experienced, and never smelled.

I shook my head with confusion when something moved my soul, lifted my heart, brushed up against my spirit, and then carried me to where I was standing in front of the mirror.

There, I opened my eyes and saw my reflection looking back at me. The image in the mirror spoke: "I am the God that you have forgotten."

It said, "You will always be a direct descendant and cocreator of all there is and of all there will be. You are an infant of the cosmos transcended by the Creator."

I fully understand the transformation of humankind, knowing that I am because there was never a time when humankind was not—coming into physical existence once, moving from the invisible to the visible, the essence of life. That image in the mirror now looking back is the image that acknowledges the whole of who I am.

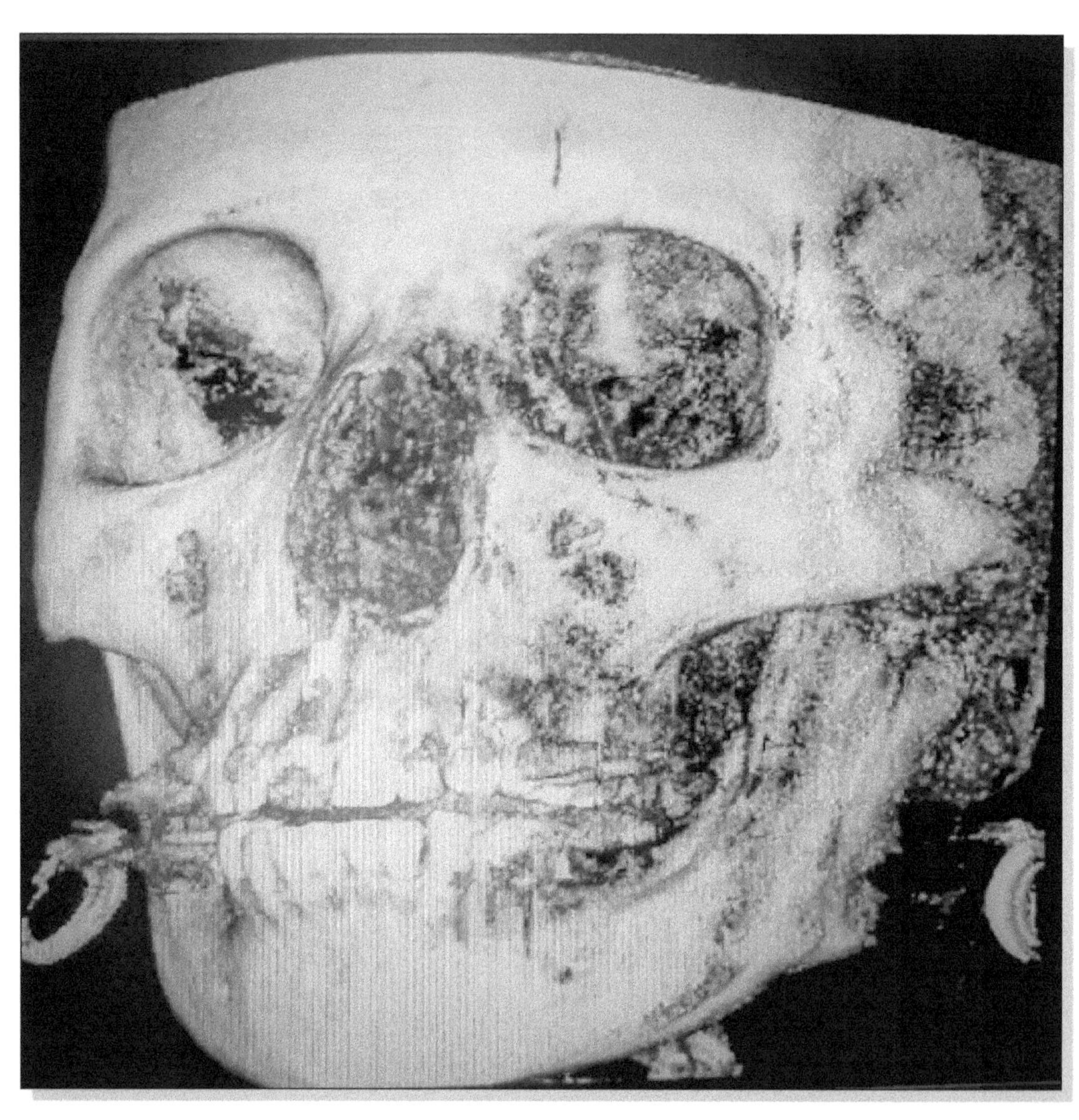

A DECISION MADE

When you decide to kidnap a child, you take him or her away from his or her biological family, including his or her parents.

You also take a brother or sister from his or her siblings, take a grandchild from his or her grandparents, and take a nephew or niece from his or her aunts and uncles. You have no regard for any connection with cousins either.

Your act of violence takes a child away from his or her future friends and from any future love interest. That must never happen.

Your act of violence takes away a prospective school friend from his or her schoolmates. You deny the child a relationship with a future coworker, which now will remain unknown; you remove the possibility of a neighbor offering a helping hand, or of a professional, innovator, or creator serving humanity.

Your act takes away a possible future marriage that now will never be experienced, a family line that now may not be carried on, and a child's passage through time.

When you kidnap one of your fellow souls, you intentionally decide that you are the gatekeeper to his or her life and also his or her executioner.

Whether you are or are not a kidnapper, the act of kidnapping makes you a predatory criminal.

A kidnapper is a false friend who molests, abducts, murders, rapes, and pillages. His or her infected mind is fueled by a poisoned soul.

Predatory behaviors are poison to our world, especially the kidnapping or murdering of a person of any age. These victims will remain as precious souls never to be forgotten.

PURPOSE

Do we struggle with knowing that life sometimes challenges us with truths and facts in the wake of incidents and events? We know that what we think is true today can change as we go through life and discover new horizons.

Let us therefore remember to be conscious and to be consistent in using evidence to prove universal truths.

What is the truth? The truth is that everyone in this world is a potential genius, and one's purpose in this life is to discover the gift within that has been given by a higher entity.

You were chosen and gifted. Your purpose in life is to define yourself and to give back to humanity. Maybe doing so would help the genius within you come to the surface.

How does you discover your purpose in life? By becoming aware of where your passion lies. Also, having a genuine desire to make a difference may help to pave your way, leading you to a place where you radiate the light of success, becoming an inspiration to others.

I continue to grow and open my mind to learning life's lessons. I've realized that as I travel life's journey, my purpose is revealed in many ways.

THE ATOMIC CLOCK

The atomic clock keeps track of the passage of time. It shows a symbol of a pyramid with seven steps, and on the face of each of the seven steps is a sequence of seven increments of time (seconds, minutes, hours, days, weeks, months, and years).

We plan our goals and work toward achieving them, symbolically making use of a remote control to more accurately navigate to our future.

Each digital step enables us to calculate time, symbolized by the image of a sunrise. Presented in symbols are the morphing images that show that life is constantly in motion. We have chosen to be the directors of our own lives.

Consequently, we each have only a certain amount of time to live our lives. We must know that time is certain and that we are here as visitors to this physical realm.

Above the tip of the pyramid is an image of a sunrise, with the sun energizing our bodies. There is also an image of a continuously flowing waterfall connected with a body of water, helping us to navigate our path and to maintain our balance throughout our life's journey.

For the term of a person's life on earth, an assigned executor inputs the person's birthday and the date of the his or her death. These dates define a person's life as the person passes through time. Seven revolutions of time represent a complete journey.

We should live our lives knowing that life continues to unfold and should not be taken for granted. Every day upon sunrise, we face either another day to live or the day that marks the end of our journey.

The atomic clock helps us visualize time. Or it could be used to fulfill any purpose.

A person's life is the journey taken, and this is computed in terms of the soul's energy, with the purpose of capturing the essence of the person's existence.

A person should not contemplate if his or her life matters to others. A person should know that for what he or she commits to doing between sunrise and sunset, he or she will be called to account.

FOR A FLEETING MOMENT,
THEY DID NOT STOP TO THINK

The people who feel no connection to the earth never think about the rocks embedded in the mountains, rivers, lakes, and soil of the earth. Or the coral, or the wild creatures. O the stories the rocks could tell.

People don't realize that the rocks were here on this earth before their arrival. They fail to realize these earthly rocks have been dug from the earth by men in order to build highways and byways and to make countertops, all the rocks' properties being leveraged to serve humankind.

Let it be known that these rocks that you neglect to respect make up the landmass that we walk on every day.

It's shameful that many fail to take the time to think about the trees and their leaves, the leaves' purpose, and the trees' relation to the earth.

People rarely consider that the oxygen they inhale becomes the carbon dioxide they exhale, which is then provided to the trees and all other forms of flora. People don't know that the tree inhales by way of its leaves.

People fail to acknowledge that which is made from the soil. On this landmass, there once was a people whose hair looked like the bark of a tree. And their skin perfectly blended with the colors of the forest and with nature in general.

Their eyes were shaped like the grains in the Garden of Eden. In contrast, the nuts and fruits that fall from the trees connect to the biological organs of the earth. Their blood flows in conjunction with Mother Earth's roots, existing where the soil is moist.

People don't stop to think about Mother Earth's consciousness, as they do not understand that humankind could make use of this source of energy and power. This is a transmission to connect to the more significant part of the universe and creation.

People never stop to think about the water and the many paths it takes while flowing on its journey to give itself a purpose. People do not think about the life support provided to all species, which includes the water flowing from the rocks, the soil, and the sand.

People do not visualize the blood flow of nature, the earth's precious blood flow, which is something humankind must understand. Oil for fuel is blood that is taken from the earth.

Humankind doesn't understand that nature is crying loud, feeling agitated each time humanity forces a syringe into its surface, pumping out blood from its broken veins so that human beings may use it to serve themselves and provide themselves pleasure.

People never stop to think about the sand they walk upon when polluting the ground with their waste.

They never stop and connect with the oxygen in the atmosphere that sustains both them and nature. Life would cease to exist without the breath.

People never stop to wonder about the atmosphere or how humankind has polluted the air that we breathe. Human beings never think that their quality of life is solely dependent upon clean air.

Nevertheless, human beings continue to chew on any propaganda that is fed to them, giving reasons for why they need these unnecessary things that pollute the atmosphere. People never stand for the real cause, which is to secure this vital entity, because life matters.

Furthermore, when thinking about the Northern Hemisphere and the United States, one can only wonder about the coppertoned people who rose from the soil of the North American continent. Their glory is within this Garden of Eden, which is enriched with the birth of its children.

All others come to bathe and to breathe in North America's greatness. Why do they fail to breathe with understanding and give respect to the children, the trees, the animals, and the air that sustains all life? If they create no genuine connection, then none of those visitors will ever be claimed by this soil as its children, no matter how long they stay.

Wow, just tell these types of people with no conscious connection to the earth that they should respect those belonging to the soil of the North American continent. Tell them that they are missing an authentic connection that would otherwise enable them to truly belong.

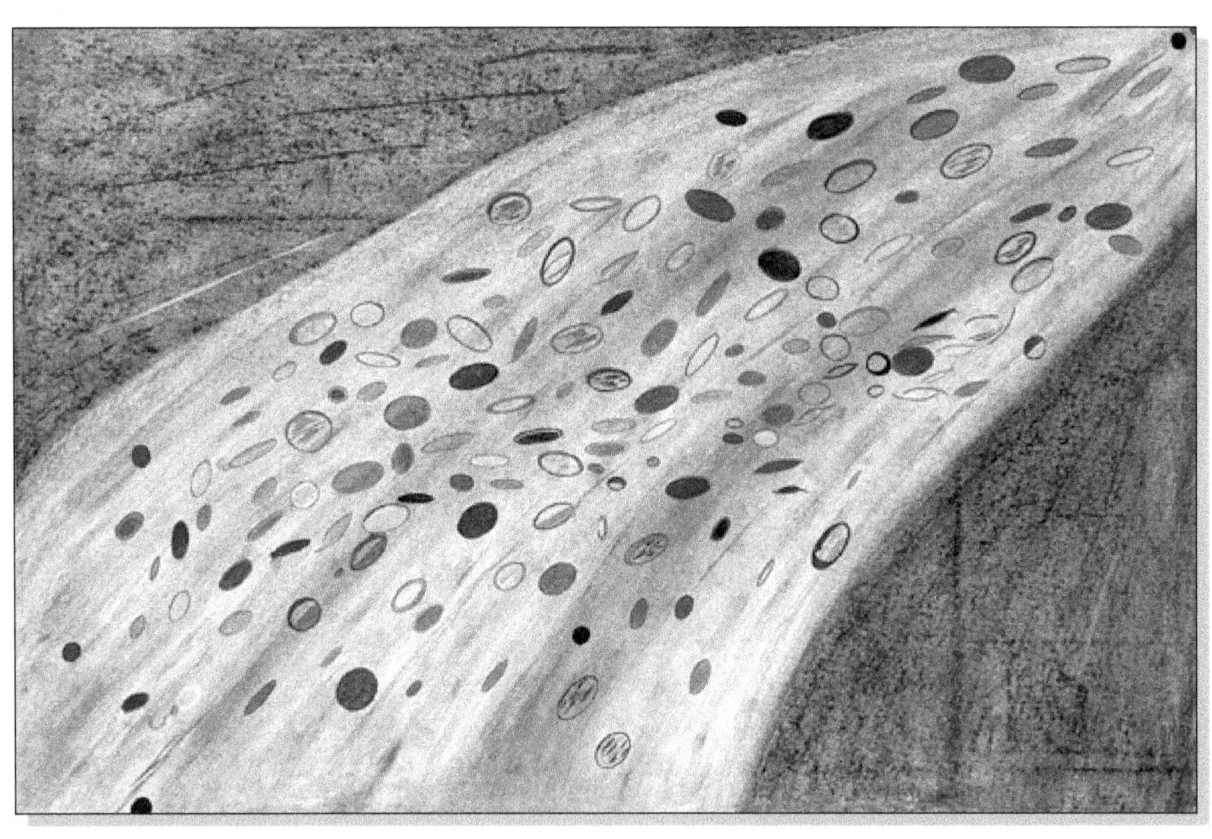

STILL TRYING TO APPLY LOGIC

"Baby-mama drama" types of people often intentionally f**k their lives up pretty quickly. Some have children without having decided to procreate with bottom-feeders. Basically, any men who act this way are just sperm donors.

Baby mamas fail to understand the science of mating. These women live lives characterized by emotional letdown. They have misconceptions about dating and are given false promises.

Some women do not realize that bearing children comes with a commitment. They fail to understand that any love they give to their children is priceless. Motherhood should involve love. It is pointless to be a mother without nurturing your children to become healthy, independent people.

These m isguided p eople n ever r ealize t hat t hey a re p lugged i nto a w eb o f i llusion. Having babies without planning for them may cause longtime setbacks and create much confusion.

Being a woman is a journey. A woman will grow with experience, then she'll know how to use wisdom. Being a mother requires a great deal of time and support. It's easier to do when a person has some help.

There is a price to pay when a woman bears a child just to trap a man into marriage.

Bearing children out of selfishness or having them for all the wrong reasons means you have no principles. Know that it will never pan out. The only thing the father will be is a sperm donor, maybe not even knowing that the woman wanted only his sperm.

It is no secret that sperm donors come from the bottom of the gene pool. Because these men have poor judgment, they will never advance to the top of the gene pool. Without a struggle, they could never survive on that more robust platform.

These freelance sperm donors have no intention of supporting their offspring or respecting the women they impregnate, not honoring them as wives or partners.

After failing to plan for a future for themselves and their children, many men opt to get out of the situation, which they see as unpleasant, and go on the run. They soon lash out at others, showing their own failure to plan and remaining unsettled forever.

Some sound advice for these broken souls: don't start a family if you are not ready to do what it takes to be a parent.

Supporting a family as a single parent comes with hardships and financial setbacks.

Your children deserve a stable home and have the right to have both parents equally connected. Your children have the right to maintain balance in their lives.

Women, your unborn child has the right to a healthy journey through life. Your child never needs to learn that you have been used a bed warmer, then used as a temporary romantic partner, if there was any romance at all.

The dogs have been called out to single you out for the wrongdoings you committed that contributed to the downfall of humankind. You have failed to care for your children by yourself, requiring the support of others who were not invited into your entanglement.

The truth becomes apparent when a child has no means to take care of himself or herself.

The child has no definite future as he struggles to find which direction is the best one to go in. He struggles while traveling down life's road, one looming with consequences.

Parents who act this way, your pursuit of temporary pleasure is missing a plan for the future of your children. They will miss out on any family legacy. Have you forgotten your responsibility to plan for the next generation?

Think before bearing a child without planning for his or her future survival. If you do plan, it may eliminate some of the negative consequences.

A child is dependent on his or her parent. Consider the decision fully before bringing a child into this world.

Loving your children is vital when preparing for their survival.

Children may not point out a parent's faults, but they may wonder why their parents failed to prepare to have a child before engaging in any misguided behaviors.

Do you care at all, or were you simply seeking to have your demands met?

Make the proper connections and the proper choices. Rely on ethics when making decisions. Think of the possible consequences of having unprotected sex if you are looking for a more positive outcome.

THE LETTER

Not knowing how to phrase it,
not knowing how it will sound,
I commissioned myself to write him a
letter to tell him what went down.

This man I thought was different
in many ways, more than one, but I
had to write a letter to get
my point across.

Why did he speak those things to me
then treat me like a stranger?

I tried to share my love. I have
I kept my promises. But just to
show his appreciation, he stabbed
me right in my back.

He lied when making me promises.
He lied when saying that he cared for me.
He even lied about his mother,
telling me she was dead.

So, I sit here to think, reminiscing
on the past. All the memories
of what we shared are just an illusion
in my head.

So, I worded the letter well,
and it sounded pretty good.
But when I got my point across,
the son of a b***h went insane.

1982

NUMBERS OF LOVE

One and one is two.
I'll give my love to you.

Two and two is four.
I'll come knocking at your door.

Three and three is six.
I need your loving fix.

Four and four is eight.
Say your loving grace.

Five and five is ten.
I want to love you all over again.

1977

I HAVE QUESTIONS

What steps do I have to take to make you mine?

What can I give you to keep you around?

What do I say to make you smile?

I just want to make you mine!

Far away in this lonely town,

praying for you and wishing for time,

I wonder what I can do to have you here.

Just sitting here thinking and wishing every day.

1981

BUT I STILL LOVE YA, MAMA

As bitter as it sounds, you attempted to rip me from the security of your womb, the womb in which I had chosen to take cover to be incubated as an embryo until the time of my birth.

When I elected to take haven there, I expected that you would have been given the understanding that life matters. Somehow I thought that I would have mattered. Yes, I was the result of one of your reckless romps.

Instead, being unborn, I misjudged the woman whose womb I chose to take refuge in. I failed to take into account that perhaps you were not ready to be a mother.

Perhaps you were misinformed, and maybe you had been socially programmed by a system that twisted your mind, making you think that your womb had no value and was not worthy enough to birth a child.

Forgive me if you must, but did you not make an effort beforehand to think on your own?

Did you not have the strength to overcome that which clouded your mind and to station guards to guard your mind so you could protect the life of another?

Did you not think that I too would come into consciousness when I was housed within your abdominal cavity?

Did you not know that I was connected to you when I attached myself to the umbilical cord, the cord that contained blood-filled veins to give me the oxygen you fed me, although it was of little nutritional value and was very unhealthy? Yes, I was there to witness it all.

Did you not know that I was connected to you, having two arteries?

Did you not know that your being pregnant with me was a gift? You did not place a value on me because life has no price tag.

Did you know that I observed your movements and your thoughts as you carried me along? Did you not know that I provided you with great health benefits as I grew within you during the pregnancy period? It was my promise in that natural setting to protect you from malevolent forces.

When I was in your womb, the pregnancy lowered your risk of endometrial cancer and ovarian cancer, along with the risk of other cancers. Pregnancy protects against certain other health problems too.

Did you not realize that I provided you with an abundance of life benefits since you carried the pregnancy to full term?

I must not forget to tell you, Mama, that your decision to end your contract with me by not taking the pregnancy to full term would have, if you had followed through with it, allowed others to use the placenta that once acted as my protector, which is one of its many purposes.

The placenta, after an abortion, is sometimes used to make marketable products. It is also used as an ingredient in many medicines.

Mama, when you thought about aborting that which was still connected to you physically and spiritually, you were defaulting on the contract that we agreed to. You had promised to carry me to full term.

But a twist of fate took place, and something changed your mind—but not your heart. Mama, you did take me to full term, and you did give birth to a healthy child.

If you'll recall, you gave birth to a healthy child whom you intentionally left to another to nurture to maturity. You managed to divest yourself of the responsibility of caring for a child. Some say that to do this is to mentally abort a child.

Many people noticed that you were a terrible parent. You failed as a mother, defaulting on your responsibilities, which remain a force in and of themselves.

If the record accurately reflects history, then around fifty years ago, in the 1960s, abortion was legal. You would have still aborted me.

You kept reminding me, Mama, that your life would have somehow been different if you had not had to take on the burden of raising me and being a mother.

You kept reminding me that you were sorry the law had not yet changed when you became pregnant with me.

You kept on reminding me that you didn't accept that I existed. You only looked at me with disgust.

You truly don't accept that I have a right to be here in this time and space. Somewhere in your lost memories, although they are not really lost, you will find that you would not stop letting me know that you had been given the right to determine my worthiness.

Yet, time has presented you with many moments to think about your own madness. It also let you know that you do not have the final say when it comes to my existence.

I know that the thought of my existence is a hindrance for you. You cannot bear to see me striving, and you can't bear to see me now, breathing right beside you.

I accept that I was the child that you wanted to bury, as then you would have been able to escape from your unfortunate dilemma.

I have since realized the agony you have suffered over the years, knowing that you were defeated in your attempt to rid yourself of this inner life.

Mama, I am not here to remind you of your faults and the deeds that you have done. It is not my duty to draw the blueprint of your life. You are your own architect.

Mama, I have since been separated from the umbilical cord, and I can now breathe independently.

My brain, having gone through the process, is now fully developed, and my other organs have developed to maturity.

You did not breastfeed me, which otherwise would have stimulated my growth and enhanced my immune system by providing me with antibody defenses against disease.

But you must know that another woman helped me, providing me with her breast milk, and it worked out well for me.

Mama, know that every time you denied my existence, I pulled through.

Also, Mama, know that every time you reminded me that you wanted to murder me, I remained. Indeed, I am still here.

Mama, you reminded me that you couldn't do this or that for me, but now I can do for myself.

Every time you tell me that it hurts you to see me since I look so much like you, Mama, you should know that I represent my own character.

Mama, you say, "You know he is not your father." You are now the mother of four other children, and you've had two abortions. One child came before me. Each of your children has a different father. You should know that I have moved on.

But, Mama, it would help if you realized that when carrying out those abortions, you suffered spiritually and opened yourself up to physiological problems and sociopathology.

Mama, every time you openly denounce me, know that my spirit is more powerful than you can imagine.

Mama, every time you remember the actions you did not take to rid your body of my embryo, house of my living soul, know that I am here now and that you have no more control over me.

The next time you decide to act in a misguided way, Mama, know that it comes with consequences.

Mama, the time has come to tell you that your faults as an absent parent have given me the strength to keep appreciating life and show gratitude for being alive. I will continue to take this journey, now being a parent myself.

Despite all the letdowns, I still love ya, Mama, as a human being.

I understand that sometimes things just happen when a young person fails to make wise decisions, not knowing the ways of life or how to navigate it.

Sadly, Mama, at this mature age, I continue to hear your whispering voice. After all these years, you have stayed true to what you said before: "If back in the day abortion was legal, you would not be here."

Mama, my final words to you are that I am still here, like many others who survived that era and beyond. We are still here.

I WONDER IF

A man I knew was charming,
but he was also known to be egotistical
and very much into himself.

But I failed to take the chance to study his ways.
Now I have learned that he went on to start a new life,
now loving someone else.

I wonder if I shall love again.
How long will it take to learn from this
experience, this hurt? Because my
love involved more than loving him.
I failed to guard
my heart.

I wonder if he thinks of me or
if he ever cared at all.

My heart became empty without his love,
and it appeared that life was not worth
living.

I wonder if I will hear from him. Or
will I receive a notice somehow or
somewhere, with him having a written
to me to explain his decision to
walk away?
Or maybe he walked away
forever. Am I ready to let it go?

Or should I spend another day
thinking about how things could
be changed?

I wonder if I will see him again.
Perhaps in a public area? Or will I have
the chance to tell him the many
ways I once loved him?

I wonder if he is happy with the
new life he has chosen, or is he thinking
night and day of the one he left
behind?

I wonder if he hurts or if
he prays at all.

I wonder if one day soon he will
walk back into my life. Will I smile
and converse with him, or will I turn away?

I wonder if his love was strong enough for
this game of life. Why couldn't
he have told the truth and put my
mind at rest?

I wonder if I will continue living and
find someone new.

I wonder if my love was great or if
he valued my time.

This man I loved has gone his own way,
leaving me completely.

I wondered then, I wonder now, but I
I will not wonder forever.

1982

PASSAGE OF TIME

Symbolic of the passage of time, the baby is on the bottom right, held by her mother. It's merely the image of the baby held in a position suggestive of a new beginning.

The image continues from her childhood to her teenage years. In her teens, we see her eyes staring at us (the viewers), which are symbolic of youth, someone trying to learn of the world outside.

Continuing into her adulthood, we see her navigating a small boat along a river, symbolizing her struggle and her search for success. As she continues to journey through the ages, you can imagine her moments in time that bring forth the fruits of her success, which she has finally earned.

The final image, on the left, is one of her older self, gazing at her past before ascending to the afterlife (symbolized by a butterfly [her spirit] flying above her).

Volume II

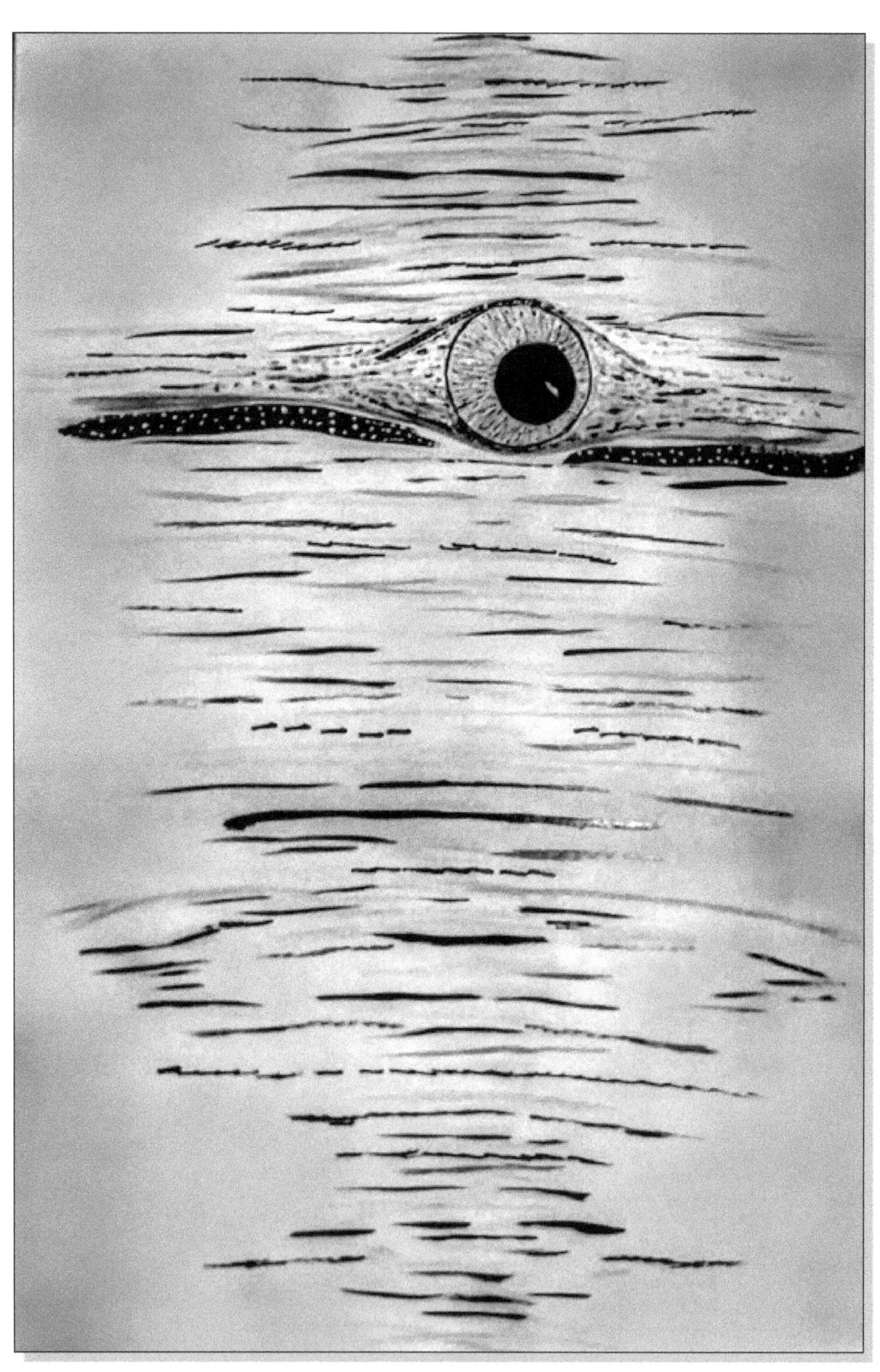

INTRODUCTION

In volume 2, I've gone within my inner self and discovered answers I'd found earlier, while letting go of that which I have already conquered. Many overlook experiences of mayhem and fail to pay attention to the problems that still block them from moving forward.

I offer these reflections and poetry not only to share my experiences and observations about life but also to invite others to look within themselves and let go of anything toxic that may be hindering them, blocking them, or hijacking their life. Often a certain memory haunts us and holds us prisoner in yesterday. Try not to be a correctional officer of yesterday's pain.

LIFE 101

My whole life has been great. I draw my breath from a source some may not comprehend. The time has come for me to appreciate this life that I continue to live as I begin to understand nature's role and how it interacts with me.

I graze and dance beneath the sun. I walk in the shadow of the sunrise or the sunset, having another day to share what I have learned and taking a moment to reconcile myself to the fact that that I have failed to learn some things.

As I meditate while bathing amid an evening storm, I enjoy the blissfulness of the moment when contemplating my next desire and moving about within this space and time.

All of life has been good to me. Now I appreciate its amazing wonders as I continue to take a stand, appreciating the flow of life's lessons. The problems I was once unable to solve are now ones about which I nod my head in understanding.

While sitting on a mountaintop with an aerial view of my town, I take in the majestic landmass beyond my town as people travel through the landscape. I have a similar view to an eagle flying high on the shifting breeze, way above the city and below the clouds.

I have since realized that if I fail to learn all my lessons now, I may learn them some other time.

One may gain an appreciation for all life by knowing that life presents us all with many opportunities to learn the lessons we need to learn. Although our lessons may appear to be similar, we are bound to learn them nevertheless.

Along my journey, I have come to understand how life functions and how humans work. I have clear vision to assess that which may require further action.

Life is not so big for me. Before offering forgiveness, you must put forth effort and demonstrate your worth.

All of life means something to me. I am making changes so as to generate a disposition that appreciates the things that matter. Thus, I pay attention to the little things, which used to eat away at my insides because I had no understanding.

All of life gives me purpose as I comprehend that death is not death; that life is not one's actual reality; that visions are not solely dreams; and that time is owned by no one, although it may be used as a standard of measurement. These ideas could become reality for those who want to create.

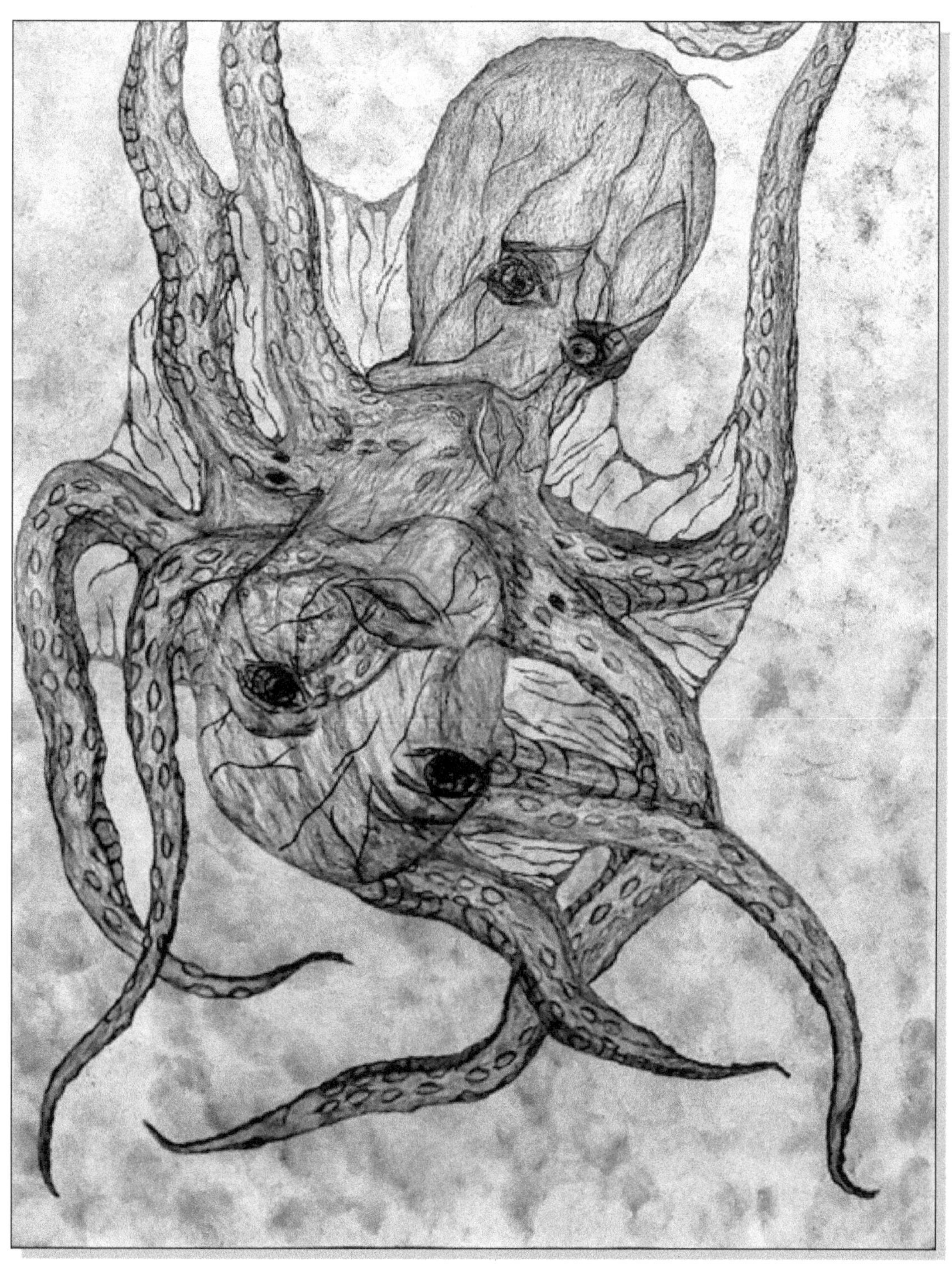

A HARD ACT NO ONE
SHOULD FOLLOW

Do I need to respect the people who demand respect even after they've demonstrated disrespectful behaviors? Do I need to respect the people who insist on prostituting themselves by climbing the corporate ladder to success? Do these people deserve respect after fornicating their way into their current positions?

These are the people who refuse to compete on a level playing field with qualified competitors. They often play dirty and take shortcuts, thereby short-circuiting the real competition.

Some of these individuals are so desperate to rise to the top that they sleep with their married boss or else lower themselves and beg for a position. Often, even though they think their actions remain hidden, people at the office, in the community, and on social media gossip about them, sometimes posting pictures or video footage.

Do these opportunists think that no one will find out that they slept with someone in exchange for a position in politics or some other high-ranking position? As position chasers, these people unscrupulously position themselves and then demand that people from the rank and file honor them.

This is weasel-like behavior. People who act this way are clumsy oafs. This type of immoral behavior exists all across the world. People study what others value so they can leverage that information and get themselves promoted. Impregnating someone else in the darkness, behind everyone's back, just because you can, comes at a cost.

Some people prostitute themselves in order to get a better a job, and this destroys their families. These opportunistic parasites cause hardship for better-qualified people. They need to be put on notice and be held accountable.

Should I have the right to abort a baby when I engage in irresponsible fornication practices? Many have agreed to have sex just to advance their careers. This is unacceptable.

Some people brag about how clever they are in leadership endeavors, but they are delusional. They need to be put on notice.

In terms of morality, a person who sleeps his or her way to the top is short-changing others, denying them a fair chance, knowing that they themselves have no regard for fairness, being opportunists. The people who behave this way should be called out.

Many at my job-site and other locations know of people whose behavior has caused others to be devastated. This forces us to reassess what represents true leadership. Many question the rules at their workplace when having to face this leadership style.

Some leaders continue to give commands and directives to others when they do not respect the people who carry out their directives.

Many question why a certain woman remained an employee at my workplace. Why did she not file a lawsuit against those who engaged in the type of behavior I am describing? Although many states have abolished this type of lawsuit, some states allow a person to file a suit against a "home-wrecker." This woman suffered after the loss of her children during pregnancy. Sadly, she could only look on, seeing the nullification of what could have been. No one should have to carry such a heavy burden. Life is irreplaceable.

Many over the years have looked on in horror, also giving newcomers warnings and teaching them about real leadership.

The type of behavior I am condemning should be called out if it causes a wife to lose her husband and, because of the hardship, miscarry her two unborn children because of the stress brought to bear on her. The third person, the outsider with no contract of marriage, knowingly interfered with the marriage by initiating a sex act with the woman.

What about the wife being an innocent bystander, later learning of her husband's unfaithfulness? What about the loss she experienced?

The memory of behaving in such a way with a man who was not her lawful husband, but her boss, will forever haunt her. Let's just say that some things are not so easy to forget, especially for someone facing the same dilemma day after day while remaining with the company.

Did anyone ask about her well-being? After learning of what happened, her spirit became troubled. Did the individuals involved think for just a moment whether or not the wife mattered? When a situation like this is made public at one's place of work, not only does it put a strain on the woman, but also it causes what was once called a marriage to become an embarrassment, laid open for others to view.

Committed employees carry on with their day-to-day tasks when given the command to respect their leaders. It is fair to say that many employees suffer in silence when trying to tolerate this type of behavior.

As a colleague, I commend this woman for having had the strength to stand by, knowing the woman who'd had an affair with her husband. It is commendable that she forgave her husband, which required a great deal of strength. She stayed vigilant and chose not to cause havoc at the workplace, continuing to work at the site where her husband and the other woman had had sex.

Should these types of people be honored, or should others spread the word of their misdeeds and their immorality? Should they be called to the carpet for abusing their positions of leadership?

Can a person reasonably stand as a leader when he or she is a liar and a deceiver? Can employees continue doing their work amid such a huge distraction in the workplace?

The problem with this type of behavior is that those who witness it must decide whether or not to stay at their jobs. And if they do stay, they will have to overlook these types of people. In any event, people will continue to judge spitefully.

One should not voice one's opinion in public if one wishes not to attract judgment or endure consequences on the job. However, behind closed doors, one has the freedom to judge as one pleases.

Depending on your employment position, if you participate in this type of behavior, you should tread lightly and refrain from gossiping with your colleagues about such unpleasant situations. Create a thread on social media to call out such behavior with the hope of stamping it out. The people who use sex as a tool in the workplace deserve to be publicly humiliated for sparking fiascos. Furthermore, the people of the world need to hear about these things. The world needs to become aware of these human vermin.

Remember, like parasites, vermin are toxic, disgusting, and obnoxious. They are similar to cockroaches, but then again, cockroaches serve a useful purpose.

Message

The author, upon learning of the aforementioned type of behavior in her own workplace, developed a distorted view of her work environment. The people who engage in such behaviors at work create a poor working environment, when the workplace is supposed to be a place for mutual respect.

Food for Thought

The behaviors described herein should not be tolerated under any circumstances. We must assess how these behaviors affect people in the workplace and others, either directly or indirectly. Should we consider removing the people who act this way from positions of leadership for the greater good? Perhaps a review board at your workplace could put an end to this infectious behavior, leading to a healthier environment.

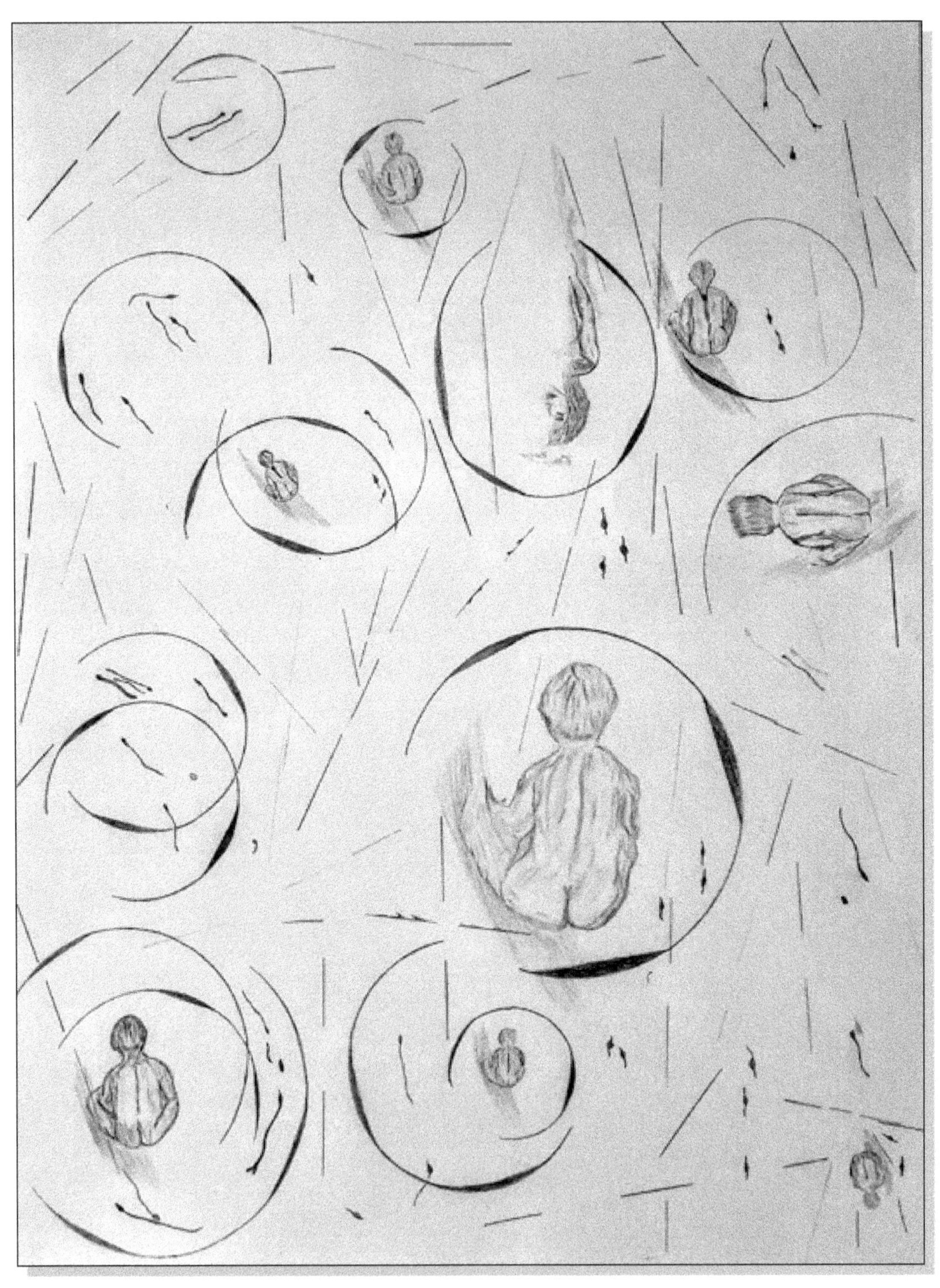

W-O-K-E

A new revolution has led to a new beginning for Black Americans, people of an exceptional race, who are taking a stand, anointing themselves, and ensuring their own survival on this planet.

These people have heard others saying that every time a black person enters a white establishment, the white people chuckle at him because they don' t know who he is.

This chuckling will turn into frowning when white people realize that black people have not forgotten that they are the co-creators of life.

Black people will no longer permit white people to use them as commodities, as black labor often leads to the growth of white capital in our society.

These giants are now awaking from their sleep with the primary purpose of teaching and of mastering life. They know how to regain the lead and secure a place for themselves.

These amazing people know the ways of business and understand how it works. They know what to do now that they've awakened, and they acknowledge what they have created, thereby knowing their true worth.

Ask the white people if they are still laughing at the great black people who have created or helped to create many things, including things from molecules.

Black people have not forgotten the science and are ready to correct their course and make use of the skills they temporarily set aside. Within a statutory reclamation period, black people will reclaim what is theirs and rebuild their communities so that their greatness may continue.

Black people warn white people not to laugh at them, as white people put them to sleep instead of allowing them to learn the things they should know. Black people have since realized that their sleep was induced.

Now that black people are woke, things will be different from how the world thought they would be. Know that others will not have to teach black people or beg them to awaken from sleep.

Although you may have been asleep, the day has come for the mountains to move mysteriously, taking everyone by surprise, the mountains being the great force that will conquer those who sleep.

People show their ignorance by continuing to rob those who are woke of their worth. These people do not understand just how senseless they are, not caring to put faces on the people whom they keep replacing, with many not caring if their replacements are undocumented aliens.

People should know what it costs to replace these people. As the giants take a stand, they will remain the greatest creators and cocreators of all.

Perhaps those who laugh at black people make a mockery of themselves, knowing that the time of bait and switch has ended. There will be no more mocking of these people for purposes of entertainment. Reality has opened the doors of the masters, and their consciousness has reached a high plateau.

Tell those from afar that while they remain on this land, hoping to take advantage of those who were once exploited, the situation has been rectified. Tell them that if they ever act this way again, they will have to pay for it.

The overlords are now telling people that their bank accounts are depleted. They took the opportunity to exploit and abuse Black Americans, and now they will be brought to account for their atrocious deeds, which are now part of the public record.

Tell everyone who has entertained themselves by telling lies about these exceptional people and their hopeful fall that they will shed tears once the supply of the goods they normally sell for a profit has been halted. Tell them that the giants have taken their rightful place.

The giants were previously programmed into servitude, and later they were encouraged to enter the service industry, serving others while neglecting to care for themselves. Someone or something that has been programmed can be updated. Take notice that the programming has been reversed.

No longer do these giants depend on a government that controls them, because they know how to respect themselves.

The programming of those who once were lost has ended, as these people, previously forced into servitude, have now stopped serving others.

People should not laugh at black people without first understanding that they used to be dependent on government because they were in need. Now the government owes them a debt that has long been in arrears.

These giants have heard the hate spouted by others against them, with most of the haters having no reason to hate.

Black people used to believe in loving others before loving themselves, but this too has shifted, and now they love themselves first. They stand tall and are opposed to being marginalized by a system that deprives them of their humanity.

One purpose of the woke movement is to bring about the reversal of what is otherwise planned, namely, the deliberate destruction of black people, whom people used to point their fingers at and blame for their own demise.

Those speaking out against black people for not fixing their own problems while they themselves fail to fix their own problems know that these people are out in full force, prepared. When the fingers stop pointing, follow the money trail and calculate the debt still owed.

People are woke when they recognize that their children, and their children's children, and the generations beyond will enjoy a promising future full of prosperity.

It may not have been televised when money stopped pouring into white communities and instead went toward rebuilding black communities, which had been destroyed.

Those who once couldn't have cared less about their own well-being, let alone their own survival, are the same people who now are showing resilience and taking care of themselves.

The world has taken a front seat to watch as black people become woke and begin building businesses and brands of their own, thus providing themselves with a way to gain wealth and leave a legacy, knowing the consequences of failing to plan.

Whites may continue to laugh at this exceptional racial group, who continue to invent things, contribute ideas, and do other wonderful stuff.

Black people see others laughing at them every time they send in a college application, although their ancestors are the ones who built the very universities they seek to attend.

Everyone should know that black people are thirsty to educate their own children and that their teachers will not deny, cover up, or ignore facts or history.

Tell black people that the days of begging for equality, after being systematically robbed, are over. The veil has been lifted, and black people now see how whites have distributed the wealth they helped to create.

Woke means creating one's own reality and not allowing outside entities to do so.

To be woke means to control the means of protecting one's own community and not allowing others to manage it.

Those of the woke movement have stopped wasting time trying to convince others to leave the plantation of the mind behind.

To be woke means to set a solid economic base, ensuring that black communities are complete with businesses, banks, educational institutions, hospitals, a political system, and politicians who address their needs.

To be woke means to own who one is and be identified by one's nationality.

Woke means not allowing the color of your skin to determine your worth.

A woke person is one who has stopped thinking that he or she is not good enough, having failed to even ask, "Not good enough for whom?"

Woke people hold positions as soldiers, warriors, leaders, patriarchs, and matriarchs, not allowing others to tell them to do otherwise.

To be woke means to love oneself and not apologize for it.

To be woke means not to allow billionaires to masquerade as benevolent people.

A woke person is one who takes care of his or her own family without making excuses for failing to do so.

A woke person is someone who could care less if others spew hate and act hatefully toward them. A woke person refuses to give any power to words of hatred or discrimination.

A woke person is someone who will identify, locate, and deal with the race traders and politically motivated assassins who are working against her racial group.

A person who is woke will not allow an enemy to marginalize him or take ownership of his soul.

To be woke means to overtake the current leadership and claim their inheritance.

Woke means not allowing others to indoctrinate your mind.

Woke people reeducate themselves after realizing they have been programmed and indoctrinated by the very people who once were their conquerors.

Woke means not allowing someone to take a dump on your floor, claiming to have thought it was a toilet.

Woke means choosing not to fight others' causes but instead standing up and exercising one's own Second Amendment rights.

A woke person understands that committing an act of violence against herself is the result of her having been programmed to hate herself.

A woke person knows that the black population is controlled by eugenics.

Woke means knowing that there has never been a period in history absent a fight for freedom.

A woke person knows that people of his exceptional race have no birth records, their being made of the same material as the universe and knowing that they can procreate.

Woke means not allowing someone else to represent you and forbidding any outsiders from stealing your identity, including your fashion sense and grooming habits, then claiming that they can do a better job than you of presenting the concerns of the black community.

We need to empower black people. We need to separate black communities from other communities because the former is in need of political and economic recovery. These communities need to control their own economies and thereby achieve equality.

Yesterday, white people used to laugh at black people, saying they lacked self-respect. Today, black people are reassessing their principles while building lives for themselves. They have resurrected morality and social standards, showing their will to survive.

Black people are gaining the strength needed to survive on this planet and build their own establishments. There will be no more talk of black people kneeling down to scoop up the handful of crumbs thrown at them. The time is coming when black people will have the last laugh. People are beginning to see that not only are there documents proving that certain black people throughout history have achieved excellence, but also that some black people today are achieving excellence.

Woke people are no longer asleep. Their eyes are now open to the strategies used, including lawmaking and redlining, by white people to keep black people asleep so that the whites can finally gain total control over the blacks.

Woke people know of the strategies used by the United States government to eliminate the true aboriginal people of North America.

A woke person realizes that the government continues to divide and conquer, dividing people of all nations to keep them docile.

These people are now awake and will not accept any token gestures, including being offered dead-end jobs, nor will they allow the internet to distract them from rebuilding their communities. They will not allow themselves to become entwined with anything that prevents them from taking steps toward self-empowerment.

Black people stand against the white people who try to trick them with illusions, spouting some philosophy about everyone getting along, saying that one day things will get better, just please keep getting down on your knees and praying.

Know that black people have gotten up from their knees and are now taking their power back, no longer resigned to begging.

Black American enslaved were once the most valuable commodity on the U.S. stock exchange, but the days of ignorance, that is, of making money off the backs of enslaved people, are over.

Go ahead, keep laughing while more and more black people begin to patronize black-owned businesses exclusively—clothing shops, supermarkets, restaurants, medical centers, and so forth—and completely stop supporting white-owned businesses.

Woke means returning to nature and learning about agriculture.

Woke means walking away from everything and doing for oneself.

A woke person knows when enough is enough and that payment is owed, as the labor of black people was once used by white people to create wealth.

Woke means knowing how to identify those who intentionally mislead others for profit.

Woke means having a purpose as a people, safeguarding your human rights, and understanding civil law.

Woke is taking a stand and knowing how to govern yourself and protect your community. It also involves lobbying and putting in place a home-rule charter.

Woke means to refuse to be a test dummy for others to run experiments on.

Woke people are not apologetic for who they are and accept their true identity, history, and culture in the land where they live.

Woke means knowing that the Out of Africa hypothesis is just propaganda intended to control people's minds and disassociate Black Americans from the land of their birthright.

Woke people know that they were never poor, only misinformed, after having given their trust but then being swindled.

To be woke is to realize that all the lies that could possibly be told about you have been told and that the time has come for you to confront the people who spread those lies.

To be woke is to stop carrying the load for white people .

Woke means rebuking with a loud roar those who claim that they will remain in power on this planet for the next five hundred years.

Woke means knowing when someone is interrupting you just so they can derail your thought process and begin denying the facts.

A woke person is someone who is ready for any potential outcome.

People are woke when they begin doing for themselves, breaking the chains on their consciousness.

To be woke is to create a political party representative of Black Americans and to find a way to support it.

To be woke means to develop a legal system specifically for black Americans, one that protects black commerce and ensures justice for all.

Woke means getting on task and staying on task, eliminating any distractions, and creating an agenda.

W-O-K-E—Working on Creating an Economy

Woke means being consistent.

Woke people realize they have been systematically attacked for centuries.

Woke people know that their communities have been occupied and that they themselves have been bound by a negative force.

Woke means starving out those negative entities.

To be woke means to stop letting others assess your worth.

Woke people direct their own destinies.

The black community is woke because black people now support black-owned establishments to ensure their place in this land and on this continent while earning money to secure their future.

Woke means never allowing the nightmare to recur.

Woke means to rise up, as opposed to being annihilated.

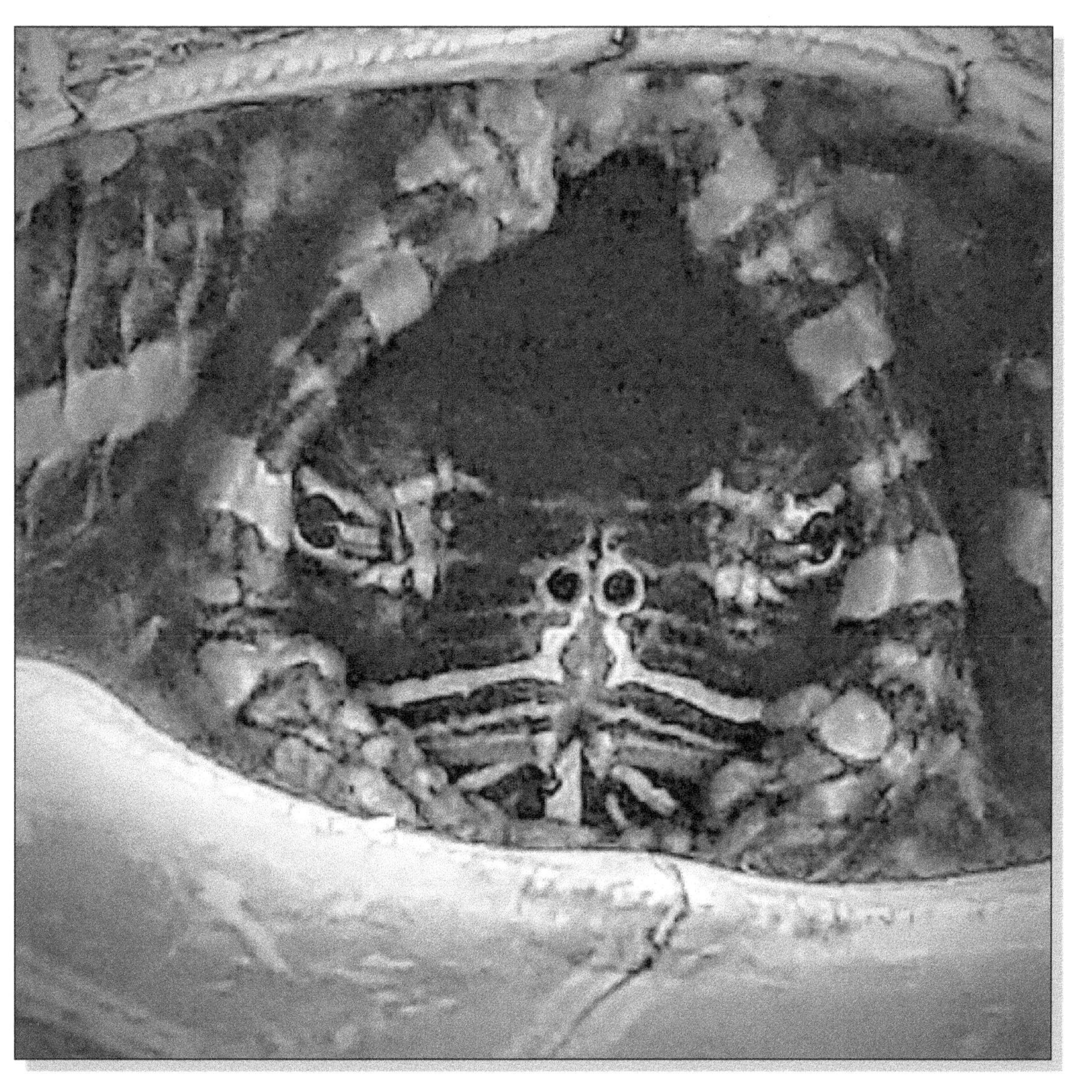

WE KEEP LAUGHING AT THEM

Every time we see a black person enter one of our establishments, we chuckle at them because they fail to grasp who they are.

Everyone knows they do not understand how business works. They don't realize how to take advantage of the time and space they have, and they do not acknowledge their true worth.

We keep laughing at them even though we well know that they were once a great people. We acknowledge that they have contributed to the creation of many things, including life molecules.

Because no one remembers the black scientists who made certain discoveries or the black inventors who created something new, other people laid claim to these things. But now the statute of limitations has run out for white people's claim on such items.

We laugh at black people because they sleep when things they should know are being talked out. It is not our place to teach them or to beg them to wake up from their hypnotic state.

We laugh at their ignorance while continuing to rob them of their worth. We cannot help but fail to grasp the full scope of their senselessness, not caring to put a face on the people who keep replacing them, with many not caring if people come from abroad to do so.

We cannot stop laughing at black people when we see them making a mockery of themselves. The world knows them as the once great ones, yet they keep trying to mimic others.

We quietly laugh at them, giving them the illusion that they are inferior human beings, when we know that our human lineage began with them. Yet, we graft our story of history onto the real story to maintain our dominance.

When hearing about these people from afar, we learn of their exploits and adverse behaviors. We refuse to shed any tears for them or perform any act of sympathy toward them as they move downward toward their demise. We have now taken on the role of replacing everything that they keep denying.

Having studied the situation, we now acknowledge that black Americans were programmed into servitude and then encouraged to serve everyone else, neglecting to care for themselves. We see their constant dependency on the deep state government, which controls them like a flock of sheep while they continue to disrespect themselves.

We have witnessed the hate among them. Nevertheless, black people are sure to love others. However, they do not understand why whites continue to disrespect them.

We are here as witnesses to the many atrocities that have contributed to the current plight of Black Americans and their destructive behavior toward each other as they repeatedly blame others for not fixing their problems while they fail to fix those same problems themselves. Or do many use hatred toward each other as a form of escapism?

We will continue to laugh at them, seeing them as too willing to please others, thereby providing others with a revenue stream, leading to wealth.

Anyone can see in the media that money pours out of black communities and straight into the hands of people who could care less about their well-being, let alone their survival.

The world has front seats to witness their demise as they continue shopping at white-owned businesses and buying white-owned brands. Thus, black people freely provide a revenue stream to others without knowing the consequences. One consequence is that the money goes toward financing the genocide of the black race.

We laugh at black people when they apply to white colleges, while black colleges remain in a state of disrepair. Ultimately, black people don't know that their first university is their mother's womb.

We keep laughing at black people when we see them begging for equality and for equal representation in politics. They forfeited their opportunity by not seeking to empower themselves to separate from the white race. Most importantly, black people need to control their own economies; then they'll achieve separation and equality.

Sadly, they continue begging to live amid those who continue to despise them.

We laugh at black people for their failure to respect themselves. Others observe their lack of principles in building their lives, their lack of morals, and their lack of standards. We will keep laughing at them at the height of their weakness, showing no fight to survive.

They fail to know that the world is working hand in hand, tirelessly, to extinguish them.

Oh, we keep thanking them for allowing us to come onto their land, then place ourselves at the front of the food line, thanking them for letting us claim their resources and for placing our children ahead of their children.

We will keep laughing at them as they eventually allow us to eventually take everything from them, including the legislation meant to benefit them.

We analyze their behavior when they continue to vote for political candidates who make promises but do nothing for them. At the same time, they stand waiting with a hope and a dream while failing to adopt a strategy to cure their madness.

We see that their eyes remain closed to others who appear to want genocide. We must alert them to the fact that while white people remain in power, black people will have no share of the wealth taken from them but will be used as contributors to the wealth of those in power.

As a racial group, black people, we realize, do not study history but repeat it. Many blacks have seen the extermination of many other blacks.

We will demonstrate that the race for survival of all species is important.

We laugh at people for not realizing that the world is on a reset. A one-world government will control them, as all will learn that they are the actual commodities.

We white people will deny that we get preferential treatment and take advantage of loop-holes in the tax code. We also deny that we receive certain privileges, and we lie about cheating the system so as to place ourselves ahead of others. Without a doubt, we will continue to co-opt everything that was meant for black people.

When black people take to our establishments, we laugh at them, like pigeons begging for a handful of crumbs to be thrown at them.

There are records all over the world of the excellence achieved by certain black people. We know that if we allow them to excel, they will build anything, and they will make it extraordinary, better than anything that has ever existed. The world will be at fault if it wakes the sleeping giants that will overpower most of us and replace us.

However, we beg black people to please stay asleep a little while longer; after all, we do not want them to rise up and take what we now have. Yes, we insist that they stay asleep just a little longer. We need the time to get ourselves into a position of total control over others.

We promise to throw more trinkets and more useless career choices at them, also sending the internet their way, so we can observe their interactions, tap into their consciousness by evaluating their exchanges, then make plans to protect our establishments from them.

We promote the illusion that we'd like everyone to get along and that one day things will get better if people just please keep on getting down on their knees and praying.

We white people promise that we will sit together and share ideas and principles. We say that we will always take care of black people and never lead them astray; after all, they are the most valuable commodity on the stock exchange.

Nevertheless, we still hope they do not wake up. From what we have learned about those long periods of sleep, their napping is well worth any time we have invested to make it so.

We promise that we will change the human rights laws, with some calling for civil rights. This would show that we have respect for their humanity. We understand that black people require some long-term respite care.

We keep laughing at them when they support our businesses, support the technology we develop, and patronize white-owned clothing shops, supermarkets, restaurants, medical centers/hospitals, and other establishments.

We keep with the age-old ideology of mistreating them, misleading them in all areas, and routinely rejecting them, refusing to acknowledge that they are the same as everyone else.

We keep laughing as we deny them, lie to them, cheat them, and steal from them, maintaining the status quo. Then we watch as they outsource their own survival, refusing to build on their own.

Keep laughing, because black people want the world to see them as property, as slaves, as manufactured consumers—a crayon color, black—thus failing to acknowledge their real identity as Aboriginal Americans, Moorish Americans, Americans, Americans, Americans (to repeat) with a claim to the land and their own nationality. We will quieten those conversations of truth, as North America is the land of their birthright, knowing that this is their ancestral land.

Black people fail to realize that they are not separate from others in terms of culture. They should understand that they are one with others who practice the same customs.

We keep laughing at them when they infer that they think the legal system that protects the rights and the trade of others will somehow afford them equal justice, if any justice at all.

If they would only keep supporting our establishments a little while longer, this would ensure our place on their land, on their continent, enabling us to secure our future.

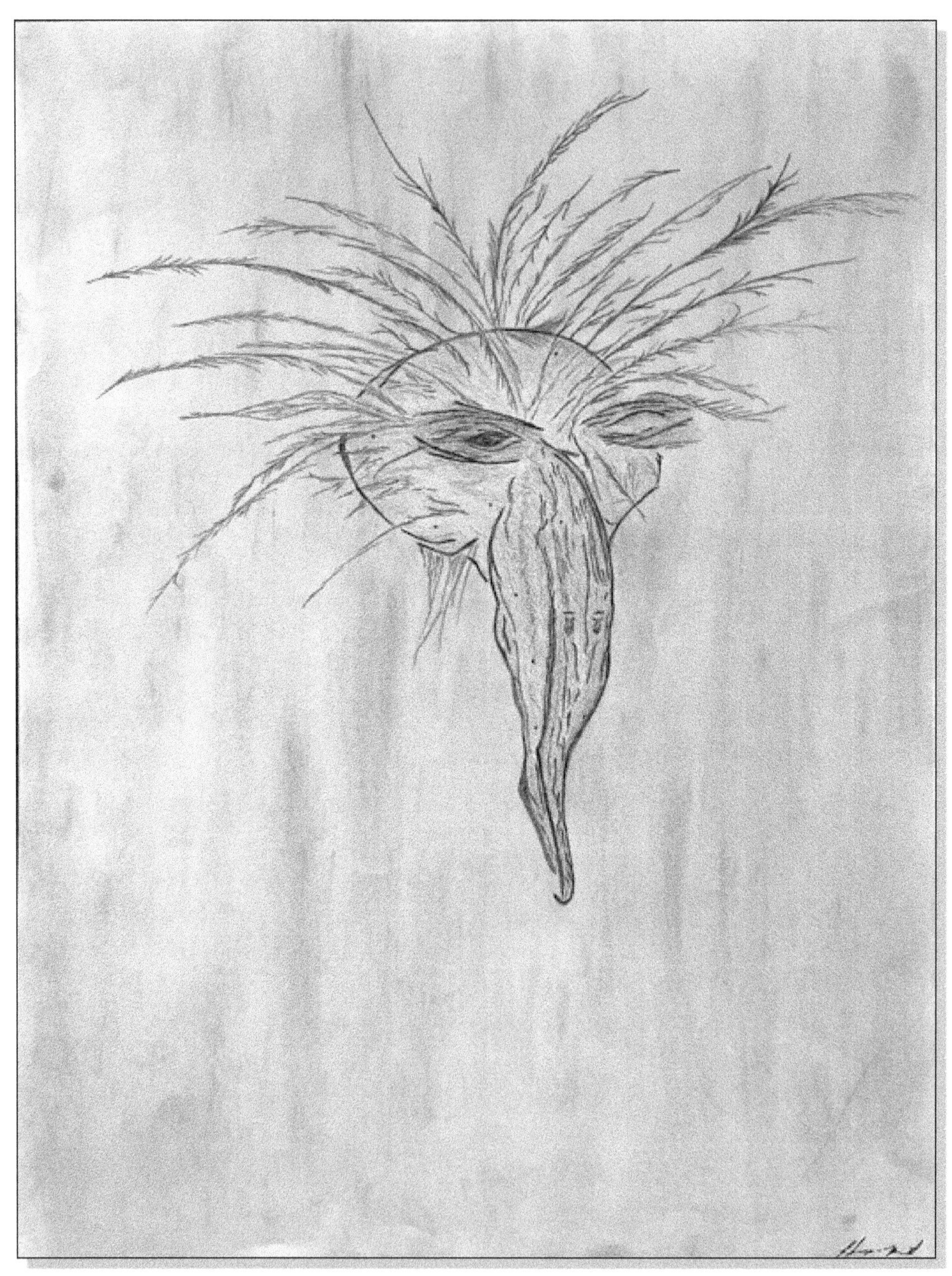

BEFORE THE END IS NEAR

Although few us think that loved ones do not matter, we should still take a stand and tell our loved ones that their lives do matter.

As a writer, I will be the first to admit that through the years I have failed to tell my loved ones that their lives matter.

As the author of this piece, I come in peace, showing appreciation and gratitude for the journey taken by a loved one within my own time. As I look back on the many years of our relationship, I can only give thanks for the laughter we continue to share, with those peals of laughter expressing things better than words can.

This loved one and I took a moment to reflect on the time when time did not matter to us. We often stayed up through the night, sharing our thoughts, gossiping about silly things, politics, or family members, and sometimes talking until sunrise about things that mattered to us.

We share thoughts about raising our children and our plans for the future, and sometimes we live only for the moment. Often, we care about nothing more than the well-being of our families and our children's future.

We cherish the things we have crafted and invented, knowing we are contributing to society. We focus on doing what we need to do to support those in need; we attempt to make a difference; and we give less time to those things we are unable to control.

If for any reason you have failed to take notice of how much I appreciate the kindness of your words, know that I notice your kindness.

If for any reason you think that I do not care for your well-being, know that your well-being has always mattered to me.

If for any reason you think that I failed to take in those life lessons and the wisdom you shared, know that I later referred to those lessons when making some decisions.

I appreciate the times when you lent me your shoulder to cry on. When I needed help figuring things out, you helped me, which I appreciate.

I acknowledge that no journey is perfect, but as we fight our battles with misunderstanding, heartache, and headaches, we manage to push through.

I thank you for your patience and understanding at a time when no one cared for me; you rescued me. When I was at a breaking point in my life, you comforted me.

Although the end is approaching, I will not race toward the finish line to say some concluding words, as I see life will continue on and that time will do what it needs to, while we spend quality time together that cannot be measured.

With time never being specific, we should live out our remaining days until our bodies are worn from experience and our minds have slowed but are wiser. We should enjoy each day until we have no more words to express ourselves and our bodies cease moving. Only then should we begin to consider that the end is near.

I say to you, my dear loved one, that until the time comes for me to make my transition and receive a new assignment in the hereafter, I will continue to thank you.

I honor you and respect you for your devotion to me and the support you have given. I am honored to have taken this journey with you, no matter how short or how long the duration; you will always matter.

Whatever differences we have, know that I respect you. I forgive you for the things you have repented of, unintentional mistakes.

Life is great, and greatness and light will always shine out from you. There is always tomorrow and the hope of another opportunity to do it all over again.

Before the end comes, know that we freely travel in peace within this vast space of time. There are no limitations on our journey. We should allow our minds to run free and not be anchored as we move through time.

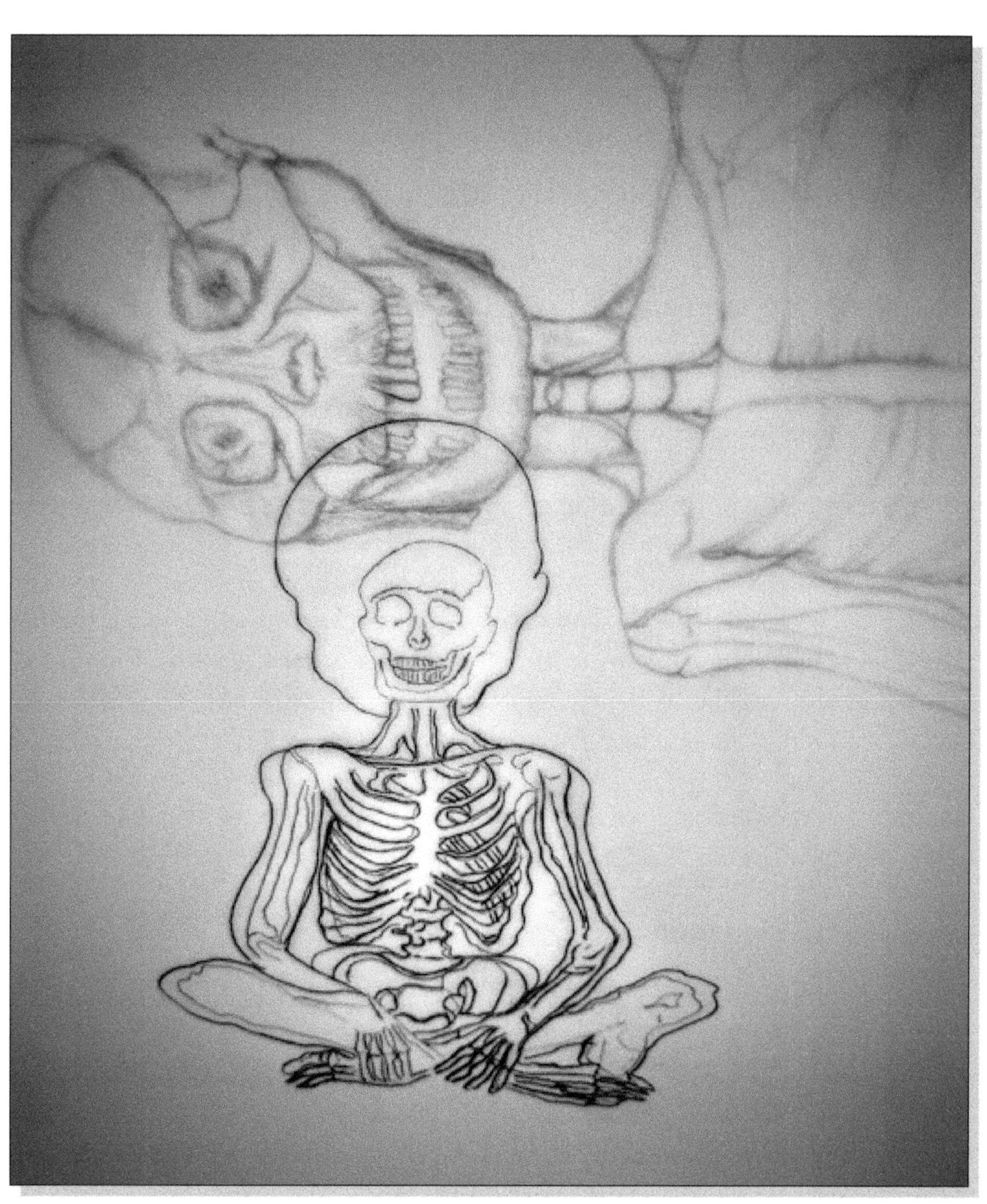

TAKING AN INVENTORY OF TIME

I struggle to find the words to express myself when thinking of a time that others believe should remain unspoken of. Still, I made an error, and now I'm taking an inventory of my deeds.

I remember when I first murmured the word *Mama*, not knowing what it meant to call out "Mama!" other than that it signified an innate connection to the woman who gave birth to me. I remember when I first crawled, stood, then walked. As time passed, life kept unfolding, bringing new developments.

In terms of the meaning of time, I didn't assume I was being recorded. I look back and see a young child laughing a lot with others. I also have some unpleasant memories.

At the tender age of seven or eight, I was posed in a posture of thought with my hands folded. As if time had stopped, I began thinking outside myself. I allowed my mind to wander into the farthest fields of life, trying to understand the meaning or purpose of life. This was something that contributed to my makeup. It also continues to shape who I am.

Yet, I question my responsibility in the process of my development. Was I accountable, accurately representing myself and showing respect to others I encountered?

Did I personally cause any harm to others, even unknowingly?

Did I help to uplift others by providing assistance when it was required?

Did I extend my support and share my knowledge, trying to enlighten others?

Did I take the time to learn about and honor those who came before me? And ultimately, did I respect myself and look after my own well-being?

Some things that I remember were difficult and challenging. Once I challenged my parents and subsequently witnessed the force of their pushback, which resulted in some lifelong lessons that may even carry over into my next life.

There were times when I was not too fond of things I did not understand. I should have shown more appreciation and gratitude toward those who reached out to me, loving me for who I was.

I quiver when thinking of the moments when I was too afraid to stand up for the things that mattered and when I failed to take the chance to walk down a different path. I convinced myself repeatedly that I was not worthy enough. That was when I was of a tender age, not yet having learned the rules of life or how to navigate it.

When I was growing up, sometimes my friendships were burdensome. I was very shy, I now see, which blocked me whenever others entered my space, although now I know they never should have been in my space in the first place.

My space is mine alone to guard and defend. This is how I allow myself the freedom to live. This attitude of mine resided deep within my mind back then, ruling out any potential friendship.

Throughout my life, I have struggled with trusting others. I have wrestled with this, refusing to be vulnerable around others and thereby give them control. As a result, my relationships were limited, and I failed to network or build a foundation. Frequently I wanted to reach out, but I did not know how to reach into that which I needed to stimulate my growth.

My mama, the woman who took care of me from infancy to maturity, made me a last request: "Baby, could you stay with me a little while longer? I don't want to die alone." I felt deep sympathy, right down to my bones.

I replied, "Mama, thank you for all you have done for me. I am grateful for your commitment and dedication in taking care of me."

I further expressed, "Mama, as much as I want to stay, I must move on." I was feeling deep grief, the tears washing down my face. I embraced Mama, then gave her a whole body hug, one full of emotion.

"Mama, your dear son, with whom I cannot bear to live beneath the same roof, will soon return to live here with you. If I were to stay, Mama, I would only be in danger. I regret leaving the only family I ever know." I said to myself, *This is something that I must deal with now, or it will come back to haunt me in the future.*

Some years after I left the home where I felt loved and protected, Mama passed. I am left with the regret of not staying and not honoring her only request. I also feel guilt, worried what Mama may have suffered after being left all alone. I'm still trying to figure it out.

My decision not to stay is a problem I have dealt with many times as an adult. It remains an unfortunate circumstance, one I've learned to live with. I realized I had to save myself.

And let it be known that indeed I am safe now. I learned later that this son of my mama, a man whom I call an uncle but who is more correctly described as a piece of atomic sh*t, contributed to his own mother's early demise. Hmm.

Time is never forgotten, only unspoken of.

When I came of age and became more aware of my surroundings, then when I learned how to navigate life, I stopped pretending that things did not bother me. When I was young, something terrible happened and I had an opportunity to save another. It still eats at my soul. My spirit knows that I did nothing.

I confess now that I looked on while a cousin died. At a tender age, when being reprimanded by his parent, my cousin was trying to escape his punishment, running through a five-story apartment building. He jumped out a window and fell to his death in the alleyway below.

But when my little cousin was running away from his mother, he ran to me for some form of comfort. I froze, not wanting to intervene in a parent's reprimanding of her child. When I froze, I failed to help this precious soul. Today, forty-plus years later, this accidental death continues to haunt me because I failed to help my cousin after he cried out loud, calling my name, asking for help.

It is something I will not forget as it is deeply rooted in my memory. I speak to his spirit, asking for his forgiveness.

This episode continues to haunt me. In fact, it kills me on the inside. I am unable able to let the memory of this tragedy go. I may have been able to prevent my cousin's death if I had not frozen.

Moving forward in taking my inventory, I will share that I was a very humble spirit. I fought with myself about the best avenue to take. I was petrified when dealing with life. It put a strain on me just to build relationships with others, especially those I did not know.

I will admit that I clammed up inside, not knowing how to love because love had not been given to me. I suffered from the lack of many things, and when it came to expressing my thoughts and feelings, my words just went unspoken.

When I take my personal inventory, I realize that I made many errors and learned some positive lessons that helped me grow. Yet, the journey was not an easy one. It meant living through times when shame reared its ugly head. I lied, saying I had not done some of the bad things I did, to show that I had some kind of importance.

Taking an account of one's life means uncovering all the little things that otherwise go unaccounted for, whether it's cheating on a test, lying to your parents about something minor, or trying to cheat time. Time accumulates with everything we do or don't do, as where we direct our energy determines that which is later manifested.

When I was sixteen, a grand-aunt visited our home. She asked me on one Sunday afternoon, "Honey, could you please braid my hair?" She said, "You are my favorite niece." In response, I said no, thinking she was drunk. I did not want to be around anyone who was under the influence of alcohol. She asked me one more time, and my response remained unchanged. Moments later, my grandfather took his sister home.

About two days later, my family was given the sad news that Auntie had passed on. I felt regretful that I had not braided her hair. My grandfather cried out loud when he heard the news that his baby sister had passed on.

I suffered from the regret of not having fulfilled Auntie's request. Perhaps she knew that she was dying, but I don't really know. Later it was discovered that a girlfriend with whom she had spent some time had put poison in her alcohol. Cherishing the memory of my auntie, I have since asked her spirit for forgiveness.

Usually, we do not have control over the information we learn from others. I was told a horrific story about a family member and his untimely demise. This was my great-grand-uncle who was hanged, and after the hanging, people mutilated his body, using hooks to rip away at his flesh, leaving his body as a pile of threads.

His family was ordered to report to the site to collect the mutilated body. This is a haunting memory for my family.

A century after that, another grand-uncle was burned alive and left at a gas station by the Ku Klux Klan (KKK). It was reported that the KKK was not pleased with one of their sisters, who had involved herself with someone from a different racial background. The family of the deceased was again called to retrieve the destroyed body.

I shared this story with someone I was trying to befriend. I had admired this person when we were younger. Our parents did not allow us to visit each other's homes. It wasn't until we were older that we saw each other again. At that time, my friend was returning to the community that had she left when she was a young child. It was a summer day, and the weather was quite gorgeous; in fact, one could not ask for a brighter day. On this day, we were together spending time in my home, but then this friend suggested that we go shopping.

The unfortunate event took place when we were shopping in a department store. It was most unexpected. My friend offered to hold my purse while I tried on some clothing in the fitting room.

After paying for the items I had selected, the unthinkable took place. Before leaving the store, we were stopped by store security. They asked to search our bags and my purse. When they did so, they found some underwear in my purse. They asked, "Miss, are these items yours?"

I responded, "No."

Unfortunately, I had associated myself with someone who did not have my best interests in mind. Taken into custody for a brief time, I was released after being questioned, serving no time. I remain grateful for the end to that nightmare and the avoidance of any embarrassment.

I never again saw or spoke to this girl I had so wanted to befriend. Life involves the learning of lessons by going through certain experiences.

I did not hate this person or wish any harm to come to her. But I did learn a lesson about making wise decisions and building a solid foundation, hopefully developing wisdom after going through this difficult experience.

Now I seek to take account of any of my misdeeds, such as failing to speak out about important things. I will start by digging deep into myself.

Another thing I will not forget are my four first cousins with whom I grew up, waiting to live out our own adventures. We learned about nature, life's building blocks, and how to share life.

As I remember, we were a close-knit pack, with me being the first of five grandchildren. Of course, I was my grandparents' favorite. I'm not bragging; it's just the truth.

My cousins and I played, doing ridiculous and silly things such as running through the pond toward the back of our property, not knowing that water moccasins / cottonmouth snakes lived in the water.

We built playhouses/clubhouses and did other fun things. Most importantly, we all hoped that our bond would last a lifetime—or at least I did.

Somehow, the wish I had made years before began to disintegrate with the separation of the pack. Sadly, three of these cousins were separated when they joined their parents to go live in bigger cities. Although their departure saddened me, all five of us remained in contact, enjoying gatherings and family time during holidays and summer vacations.

As we five cousins matured over the years, it became apparent that the separation had put a strain on our relationship. T hese young children grew and began to become independent, taking on different life challenges. T he gap widened, and we only saw each other when attending a funeral or perhaps a wedding. Everyone carried on with life, creating their own way.

But there is a twist to the story. When the three cousins were initially separated, having gone to join their parents, they remained in touch with one another, and their bond became deeper over time. But I digress.

We are adults now, with a few of us having our own adult children. However, the two remaining cousins (sisters) who remained with their grandparents never really grew up.

It appears that the pack divided themselves, creating different branches of the family tree. The three cousins couldn't care less about keeping in touch. They also didn't care if their children knew their older cousins (the two sisters).

But now these three long-lost cousins are finding their way back, wanting to rekindle the memories of their innocent childhood. Wait, did I miss something here? They want to resurrect the relationship. Why? Is it that time caught up with them? But I digress.

Sometimes silence is a great teacher. I would say that some things outside the law may also require a statutory period. I love my cousins dearly, but I honor my own time more.

Also included in my inventory are my college years. Like many, I did not take the traditional path through college. Instead, I worked full time while attending classes in evenings and on weekends. I was burning the candle at both ends, as they say, and burning myself out trying to meet all the requirements needed to graduate.

At that period in my life, I was very eager to elevate my status and learn to take care of myself. I stayed committed to my cause to prove my independence. Yet I'm sure this idea is nothing new to young adults who have no inheritance or no opportunity to go to college.

I did not fixate on what I failed to get from my parents. I stayed focused on one thing, namely, becoming successful by setting some goals.

I went on to receive an associate degree, a bachelor's degree, and some certificates of achievement for continuing education. Later, I went in pursuit of a master's degree.

Pay attention to this: I never saw any of my degrees or certificates as anything other than a sheet of paper that allowed me to get a job. I earned all my degrees just to do the one thing that they allowed me to do: work for someone else.

The primary school, colleges, universities, and technical and vocational schools I attended never provided me with the skills or gave me the required training to develop a competitive business. These schools did not encourage me or train me to become financially literate or financially independent.

So, I hustled and worked hard to elevate myself in life, only to realize that I was being held back by outside forces and also being programmed by the system to depend on others instead of myself.

My eyes remained closed for many years, not knowing that obstacles remained in my path, believing that it was the normal thing to take on debt then pay back my student loans, being left to beg another for a job. It is just that, being educated and trained to be a beggar.

Colleges are not designed to teach the masses to fish, instead existing to program students to become dependent upon others, always staying on their knees.

My older self has risen, and I have walked away from the wolves' den.

When my employment years began at age eighteen, what I perceived as truth was nothing other than an illusion of inclusion. As previously mentioned, I thought I would try to elevate myself. As I advanced in my career, I dedicated my life to work, showing absolute commitment in exchange for a weekly paycheck.

As time passed and I matured, I began to question certain things, such as the purpose of work and the reasons for being an employee. Initially, I held to the same philosophy I wrote about earlier in relation to my college years.

Sometimes we strive for things for the wrong reasons, traveling on an unknown path, until something causes us to step back and reexamine the life that we once willingly participated in.

I struggle with developing a new mindset to assess my life's purpose. This culture of working to survive is a deliberate design to keep the population under control. The program requires that one commit to meeting all standards before qualifying by way of rigorous examination and psychological testing.

Did you catch that? Not only does one have to show evidence of a college degree, but also, to gain employment, one must sit for an exam, and later a psychological exam, to prove that one is qualified for the job. Can you imagine the size of the egos of such people who devise such schemes?

As employees, we do not see the psychological exam as a requirement. It is a setup for self-destruction, having to prove to someone else that one is sane after committing oneself to years of academic study. Yet, possessing a college degree allowed me only to put one foot in the door while participating in the game of life, which is controlled by others.

My employment involved pushing papers and sitting at a desk, then later using digital devices.

I looked into some specialty careers requiring a license, a degree, or a certificate, which caused me to question the validity of a college degree.

So, how educated are we? We take out student loans that are hard to pay back. We apply to institutions of higher education, only to be indebted to a system that uses our time, bodies, and energy to grow itself. As a college graduate who had been indoctrinated, I remained in the Downward Dog position, a lifetime beggar for a job.

We should not ask how we got into this situation. Instead, we should realize that since we know of this situation, we must individually and collectively work to overcome the desire to go anywhere near the wolves' den.

Some people say that they were directed by their parents, other family members, or society at large to get into debt to receive a college education. Some of my family members told me

I needed to go to school, attend college, and then get a government job, saying that such a job would remove any worries about stability. Never did these family members encourage me to become an entrepreneur. Many were taken in by the propaganda that a college degree enriches one's life, thinking that college was the ultimate path to being successful.

I question the point of possessing a college degree, now realizing that there are additional qualifications for getting a job, such as exams (including a psychological exam), excessive training sessions, and training camps.

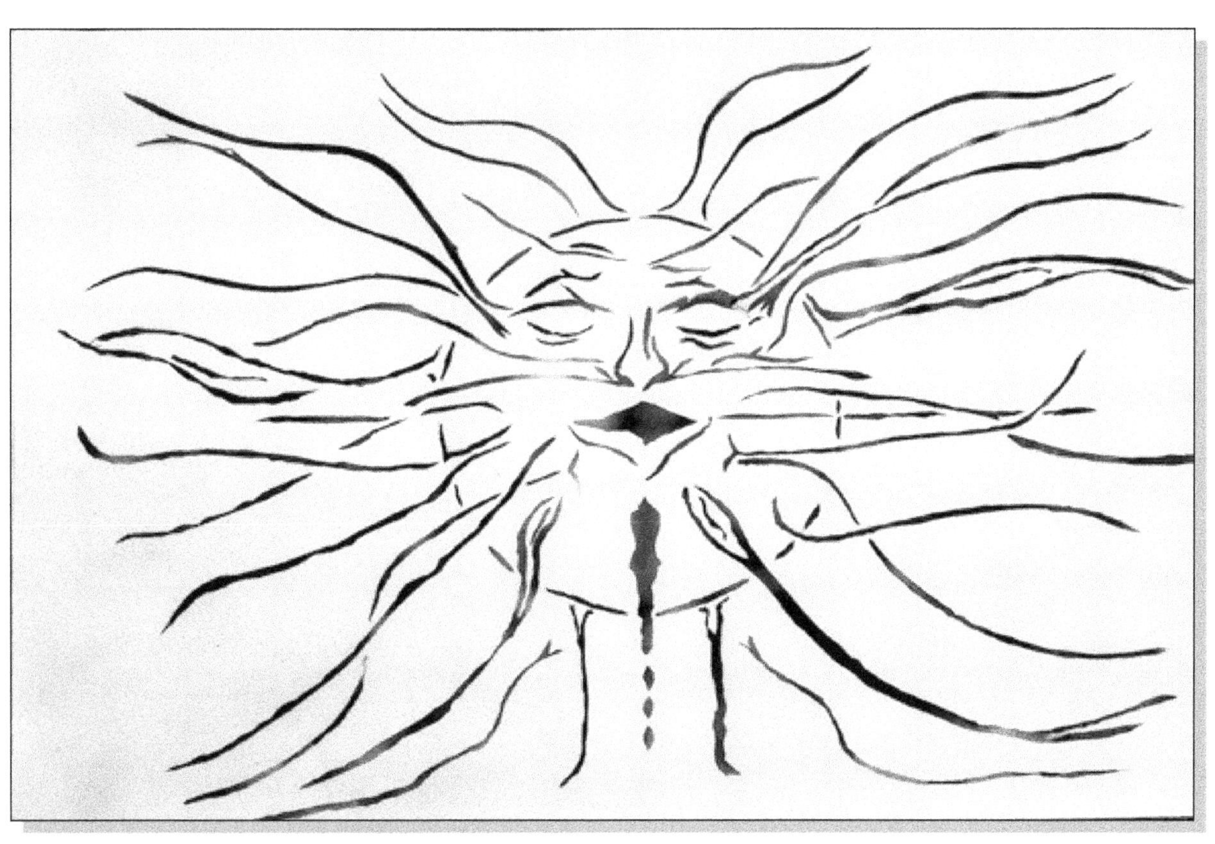

How valuable are most of these diplomas? And the point is? Can we agree that many of the skills required for certain jobs can be gotten through training without the need for a so-called "important" college degree.

After having been part of the workforce for decades, I learned that I had no voice to express my concerns. Back in the beginning, I had no eyes to see the darkness that came with committing myself to a job.

Having no voice is similar to closing your eyes to certain concerns and keeping your mouth shut. Call it what it is. I was in a job with the illusion that I was somewhat free to express my ideas, thinking that I was on the way to living a larger life. But the illusion of freedom came with a cost.

When we think about all the madness involved with employment, we see that working causes us to lie dormant, having no control over our essence. Instead, we give our power over to an establishment that will take charge of our dysfunctional selves.

Did we consent to such dysfunction, voluntarily handing over our lives to another, just so that we could have stability and enjoy whatever tasty crumbs were thrown at us, such as houses, cars, and gadgets, not to mention social integration?

While employed, an employee is permitted to take a vacation to spend time with his or her family or friends and enjoy socializing. An employee may also have a hobby or may be raising children, which takes up time.

Maybe after doing everything else required to live, the employee will have a little time to himself or herself before the clock runs out. Considering that employees have permission to do or enjoy things only on their own time, which is short, we have placed ourselves in the position of a child.

Employment, similar to college, is one of the more outstanding taker-uppers of a person's time, crippling one's ability to have one's own thoughts and ideas or to work on use those ideas and invent something, thereby becoming a competitor in the marketplace.

A person must set a goal to be financially independent. Employment, similar to college, remains something to which a great many are indebted until they get out and stand up against the system that programmed them to be biological robots, nothing more than what others have trained them to be—robotic employees.

I will experience my most glorious period when I rise up and begin to see what life has to offer. I realize that a change is taking place now, making me realize I have become the only director of my destiny.

I am taking a turn down a new avenue after having given immediate attention to those things I needed to address. I began to look differently at the prospect of employment after I asked myself a question that required an answer, namely, "Can I too be a competitor?" It is my human right to do so. I too desire to serve humanity in my own way.

I now travel more, with the world being the view from my front porch and my backyard. I no longer set an alarm clock as a reminder that I need to clock in at someone else's place of business. I no longer have to tolerate office gossip or tolerate others I have no desire to interact with. I am happy that life has given me the needed push to travel along a different path.

Life with family and friends is what matters most while I create who I am. I continue to develop my voice, regaining the strength that others once took from me as I speak out loud and stay firm on certain things in support of others.

Taking a self-inventory allows one to put things into perspective and put things together while paying attention to the things that matter. Life is the most beautiful gift. I plan to control how I live.

SOMETIMES I WANT TO

Sometimes I want to make the rain fall while I wait to see the rainbow appear within my reach.

Sometimes I sit and watch the birds fly. They give me the thought that maybe I could fly.

As I still sit to assess my life, I realize that my time travel is consciously limited to the vast space of the universe. This is an endless journey with a vibration over which I am beginning to have control.

Sometimes I wish that I could make a poor person rich, and other times I want to teach a poor person a trade that he or she could later master.

As time wears on, I am learning that I can control those things that a few men once took away but are now controlled by masses of men.

Sometimes, I wish I could master a few more tricks, but then again, it is not yet time for my transition.

Hmm, hmm, hmm, hmm, hmm.

There are many things I would like to do if only I could learn the rules to the game of life.

Sometimes I sit and wonder about things, just letting my mind wander for a while. If I would just learn some simple things about life, then maybe I could teach myself to hunt for knowledge about the future.

All the things I want in life, I could have at my disposal if I continue to upload the magic that is within my Akashic record.

Hmm, hmm, hmm, hmm, hmm.

Oh, life would not be so complicated if only I would learn to apply the simple lessons that are available to download and not just let myself stagnate.

Sometimes I want to make the rain fall, while I wait to watch the beauty of the sunrise.

I'll soon visit the moon as it rises, waiting to see nature perform its majestic wonders and tapping into the life frequency of that which humankind is unable to imitate.

Oh, what wonder to see the beauty that life reveals, knowing that humankind is everything, as that which humankind has created is a masterpiece.

If sometimes we would only sit and listen, then time would give us the answers to life, which will remain with us.

Sometimes I wait to see the raindrops so I can observe the way they fall and then take on different shapes. Life understands that we are those raindrops waiting to take shape.

Hmm, hmm, hmm, hmm, hmm.

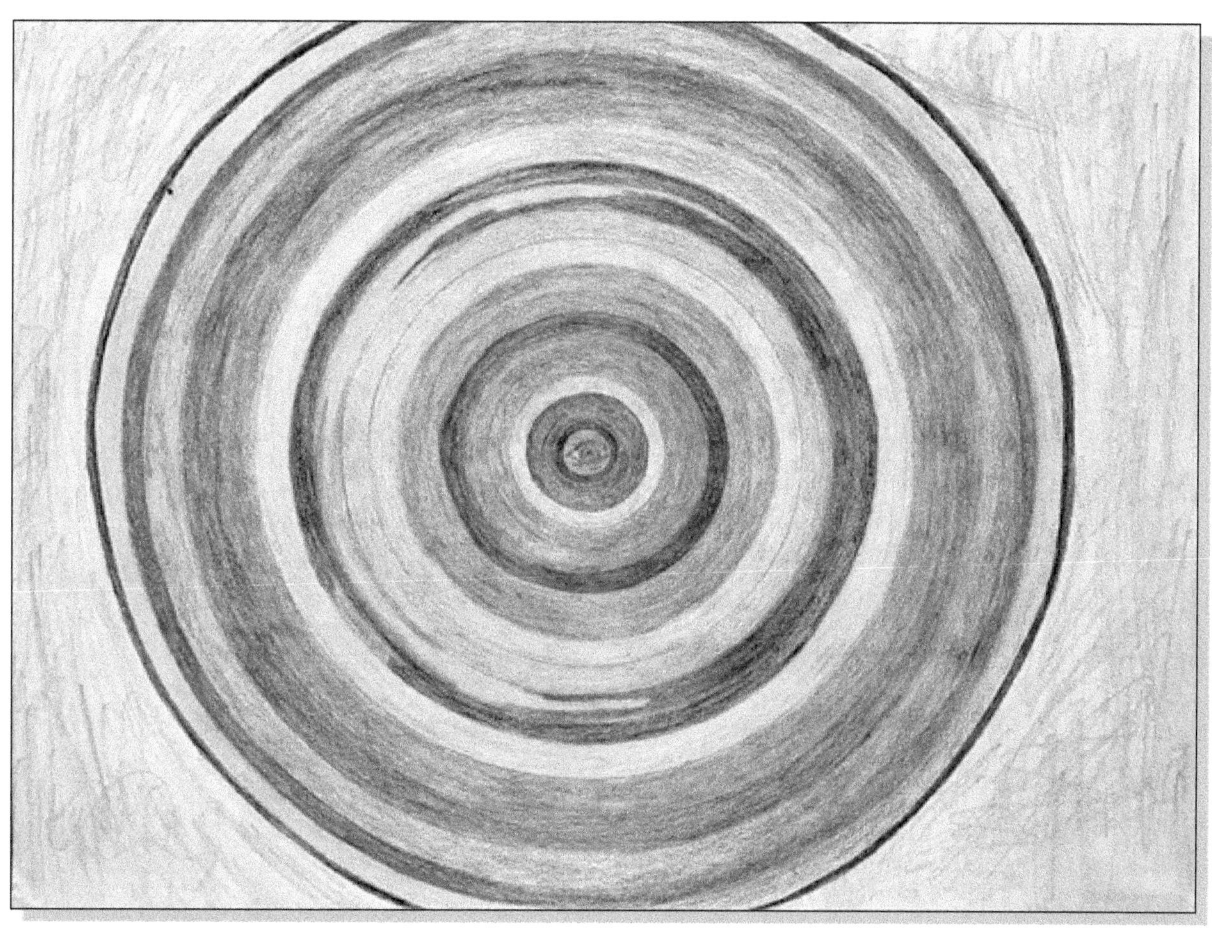

DO WE WANT TO ADDRESS THESE DISTURBING TOPICS?

Those who have chosen to engage in deviant behaviors prior to being employed at their respective establishments should be fired.

This is a look at the practice of pitting one person against the other in terms of age, sex, beauty, skin color, and hair color and texture. Society judges people based on class and education, those with college degrees being shown to the front of the employment line.

Some women, instead of fighting for their children, have resorted to fighting each other on every available platform. We have sold ourselves off to the lowest bidder and have also sold off our children.

If someone disagrees with my pro-life stance, then they are merely selfish, which fits in with the pro-death stance. These people decline to address their own concerns when siding against life in the conversation about abortion. They give no explanation.

In response, I question whether they should be permitted to discuss the pro-death position, not hiding behind a reckless pro-choice position. Those who take the position that abortion should be legal up to a week before the pregnancy comes to full term may voice their support for women to make the freewill life-altering decision to snuff out the life of an innocent entity. I said as much and received no response to my words. The conversation did lend itself to discussing the possibility of cancer and other health problems because this already reckless individual would then become more susceptible to getting cancer after the fact. Again, when I mentioned this, I received no response.

Exactly what do we want women to do? They do not realize that they are being groomed to destroy themselves by being marketed to in the hopes of selling them just about anything. I am at a loss trying to define all the vicissitudes of womanhood.

Sorry, but what is more compelling than telling the truth? Maybe people shouldn't try to describe something they know nothing about. But I must remember that we each have the freedom to speak our opinion, right?

Do some research to stay abreast of these vital topics. Keep in mind that women in the United States are not encouraged to age gracefully. Instead, women are on display, trying to remain relevant and marketable in both employment and the social arena, feeling that they must hide their gray hair, use a lot of makeup, go to the gym and exercise, wear provocative clothing, and have cosmetic surgery to remain young-looking.

Many older women now find themselves competing with millennials and Gen Z'ers for attention at work and in public. Some are competing with those not yet born.

Yes, many have been systematically programmed not to think for themselves. Thus, girls are groomed to be sexual conquests, like a forbidden fruit.

People of both sexes have become involved with the dark web, taking on deviant behaviors, wanting that which is forbidden. We call such individuals out, labeling them as perverted or sexual predators.

Most of us are guilty, but we point fingers anyway. We are the instigators who, over time, have come to accept the behaviors that Hollywood promotes and that society permits. Not enough of us have stood firm against these strong forces, thereby creating the space for these behaviors to show themselves. Many fail to voice any concern until things hit close to home.

There is a particular person whose facial expression, I see now, I should have studied more closely. I'd like to understand the psychology of those who victimize women and children. It will take more time for me to tap into this field of study.

Remember that the United States has authorized the Federal Communications Commission (FCC) to oversee and approve the content that is allowed on social media. The FCC was established in 1934 to regulate communications, namely, what is aired on television, radio, the internet, and so forth.

Hollywood actresses who are older than forty lament that it is very difficult to get work in show business. The movie and TV industry promotes the nubile female. In our country, grandmothers, mothers, and girl-children try to look as youthful as possible to compete for the same male suitors. Look at the age difference between many older male celebrities and the women they either date or marry.

We must have open dialogue. The person I have already alluded to apparently never molested anyone he had some sort of connection to. His case sounds like one of voyeurism, something that took hold of his imagination triggered by an earlier experience that made a direct impact on his mind, perverting it.

Our society must be accountable for the images and programming it pushes onto the population, although this is not to excuse other nations for not addressing these wrongdoings. Would we want to promote child pornography, either directly or indirectly, at any time? Are you kidding me? Of course not!

While sheltering in place during the communist-orchestrated global coronavirus pandemic / world reset, many were forced to remain distant from family. Many faced long work hours, keeping up with the things in need of attention, reinforcing the stereotypical roles of males and females, and placing less emphasis on nurturing, meaning there was more energy for aberrant behavior.

The individual I've been speaking about is a coworker of mine. His family will survive this troubling event. It is depressing on several levels to learn of children being abused and also learning of the manner of their abuse. The fact is that there is a market for child pornography, namely, a desensitized audience that gains pleasure from it. But we should not be blindsided by not knowing the truth.

My coworker will somehow survive the experience, which included letdowns and disappointments. Once the dust settles, he will succeed at finding a new job. Others will show up and offer their help to give this person a new start.

Many people make sure they meet or exceed the social standards for conduct and beauty, but they have a whole lot of other things going on in private.

These behaviors are troubling indeed. Are humans born with the tendency to behave in unacceptable ways, or are they learning to behave poorly from society? Does our society trigger certain odd or inexplicable behaviors?

Next, I will speak about a man who has been married for forty-seven years, having been a loving, caring father all that time. His adult children are now caring for him. For years he had a secret boyfriend, who was married, on the side. This moron had no sexual desires that were not illegal.

Our life circumstances are reminiscent of a windmill that turns perpetually, allowing each of us to experience an expulsion of air. We take in the oxygen, which permits us to stay alive, and try to exhale and prosper amid our many life experiences.

At the start of this discourse, I mentioned the difficulty of talking about these awkward subjects, even in private. Although the victim in this case will remain protected, we must reach out to those who need our support to change their unacceptable behaviors. However, when addressing the behaviors that these people admit to, we must ask what happened to them to cause them to behave in such a way.

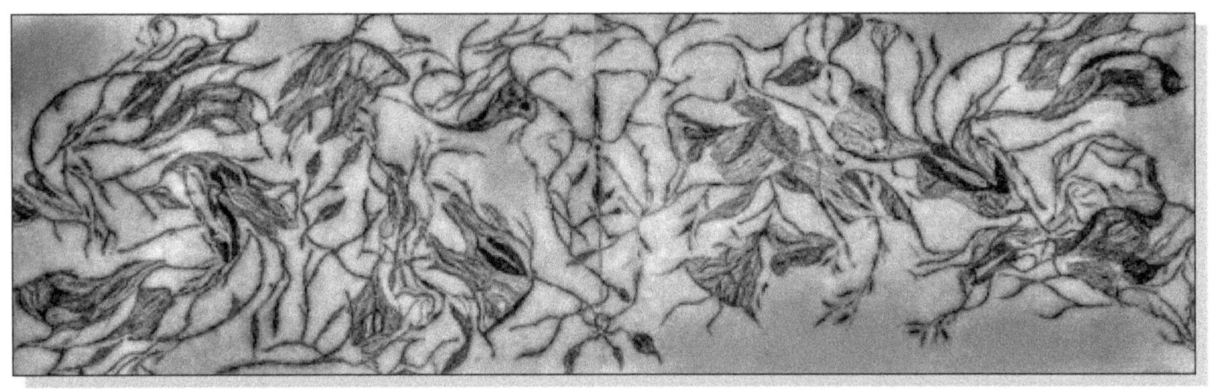

KEEP BRAGGING

Some people brag about their expensive cars, expensive footwear, valuable jewelry, and fancy attire, failing to produce the deeds of ownership to any buildings they apparently own.

They show no proof of ownership of the land that grows their food. They show no proof that the water rights are in their name, the water sustaining their lives.

These people show no proof of ownership of and make no contributions to any charitable organizations.

They stand for justice on no platform, while at the same time neglecting to prove they own the distribution centers from which their goods are shipped.

HIGH CHAIR

A baby sits in a high chair being fed by a parent. When the baby grows, reaching his or her twenties and then his or her seventies, he or she is spoon-fed more than food to sustain his or her life.

Many are fed knowledge concocted by the ruling class, who do not have the former's best interests in mind and are working with a different agenda.

When a person reaches his or her senior years—eighties, nineties, hundreds—he or she may take what is left of the time he or she has left to express what he or she failed to learn or accomplish in life.

Some people may have to wait until another life assignment to try to figure it out.

I SHALL NOT FORGET

As a woman, I realize that my mind has become saturated with the lies of others who always remind me why I don't need a man.

Some people advise me to have children without a husband, saying that I will find a man in the future.

Some people advised me to get an education so I could take care of myself.

Older women have told me that men are a dime a dozen.

They said that starting a family is not essential at a young age and that I had plenty of time to have one later.

These are the women who persuade other women to accept that they are both mother and father as they live in single-parent households.

Repeatedly, I was told by older women and some corrupted younger women that a woman does not need a man, as we make our own money. Some bragged that they made more money than many men, allowing them to take care of themselves.

I was advised not to let any man tell me what to do, and I listened in on the conversations of other women saying that no man was going to tell them what to do.

These women said that men told them they were too combative, aggressive, and argumentative, but they were equal to men in every way.

The women expressed that they had subscribed to slut culture, behaving licentiously and having no problem with being labeled with many undesirable names.

Many of these women are unconcerned about being single parents, each of their children having a different father.

They boasted about still being relevant and saying that they would have the man of their dreams after having had children before getting married.

They carried on with their conversation, expressing that they were each more powerful than any man. But many women fail to choose a decent man to father their children or to grow a family. The result of those misguided decisions was that the women later found themselves running after their babies' fathers to get them to pay child support.

I failed to listen to my inner self, unable to comprehend that the foundation of life was the opposite of the lies I had been told. When my biological clock folded in on itself, I realized that I was disenfranchised from the truth.

The truth is that some women, after falling from grace and leaving the dating pool, unprepared to be partners or wives, soon interfere with younger women's lives.

These women use many tactics, such as placing obstacles in a younger woman's path to prevent her from making healthy decisions. When older women fail at mentoring, they take on a distinct pattern of thinking. T hey become misguided mentors in terms of morals, principles, laws, and rules, engendering distrust and bringing about the deterioration of what womanhood stands for.

Bitter, they come with a vengeance to destroy a young woman's life by not giving her the proper guidance to make good choices, thus leading her to act as they do, victimizing her by encouraging her to play by their rules.

Some older women create victims of younger women to strengthen their own chances of finding a mate from within the dating pool.

This is the time when older women who misguide younger women should be called out.

Billions of dollars have been poured into the educational system, into private organizations, and into the mainstream media to target certain women and instill in them the false view that a man in the household is unnecessary.

Many women have been misguided to form emotional attachments without using their logic.

Let's appreciate those who remain as pillars through every stage of life, as life is an opportunity to develop ourselves and choose our own destiny. We are free to choose wisely for ourselves.

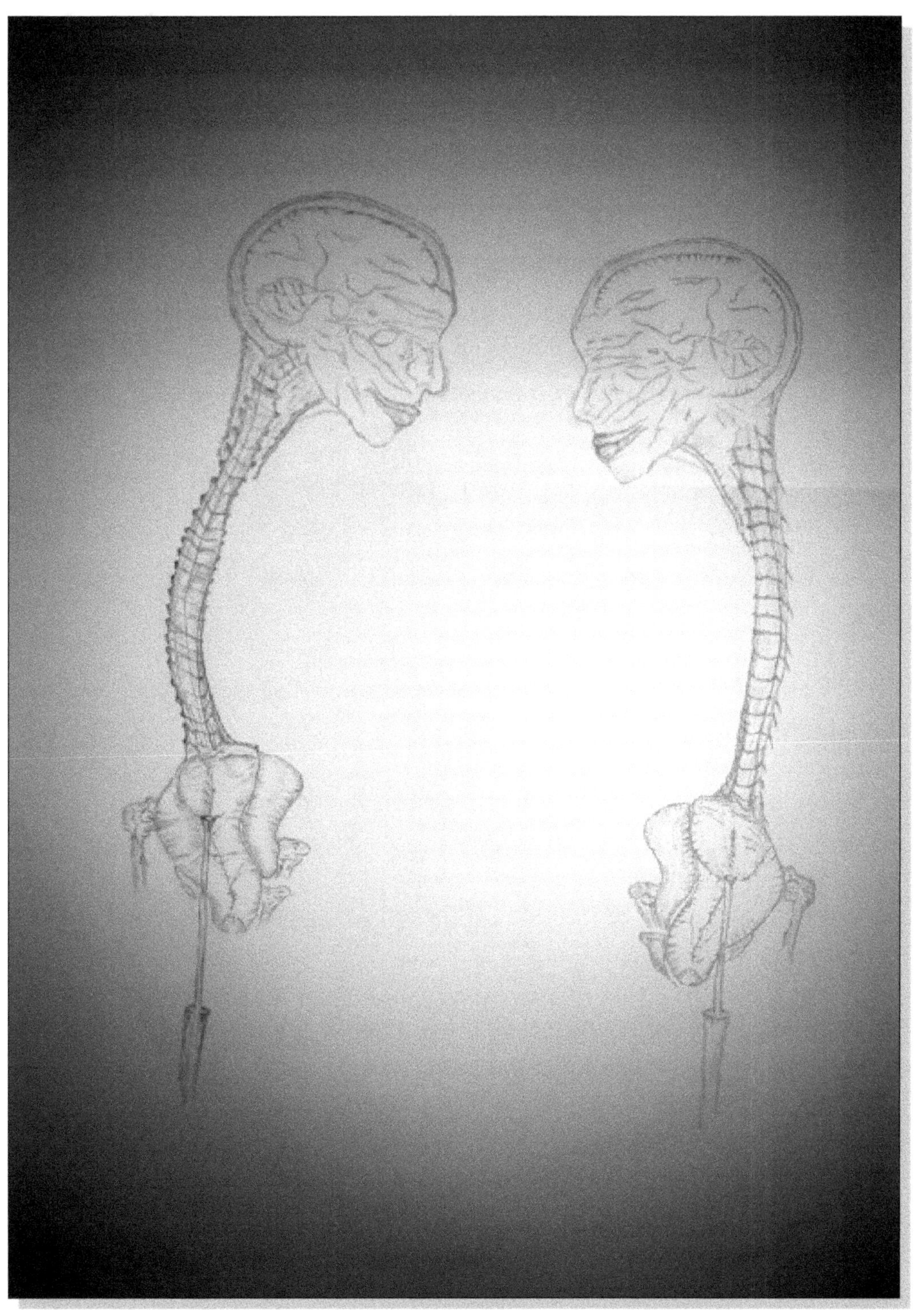

TRUTH REMAINS HIDDEN

I will deny that I have been given preferential treatment or that I take advantage of loopholes in the tax code.

I also deny others the same privileges I have, and I lie about a system that places me ahead.

Without a doubt, I will continue to co-opt everything that was meant for you.

Try not to lay the blame solely at my feet, as I am a child of a system designed in my favor that also benefits others of my kind.

Try not to blame me, as I am not prejudiced, although if I were, it would somehow make you feel better.

Don't tell me I am still receiving benefits from the wars that were fought years ago by people who look like me.

I hope you will stop telling me I should feel a certain way about the wrongs my forebears committed, then demand that I share my wealth to correct the wrongs of the past.

Sometimes I deafen my ears because I don't want to be constantly reminded of the things I'm trying to forget.

I am trying to reconcile myself to the fact that my parents provided for my future security and made sacrifices for me, which I feel I should honor.

Don't tread on my Second Amendment right to bear arms. I have a right to protect, not only myself, but also my family and my country.

So, please don't ask me to love others and hate them at the same time, knowing that I could never see them as equals.

I will not feel guilty about anything I say to anyone who attempts to make me feel bad for expressing my emotions.

I will not keep my eyes closed to the realities of life. But I will stay on task most times when the truth must remain hidden.

But if the truth remains hidden, I don't think of the imbalances between the races.

I will continue on my day-to-day journey unless I am triggered to pay some form of attention to or act on some political or economic issue.

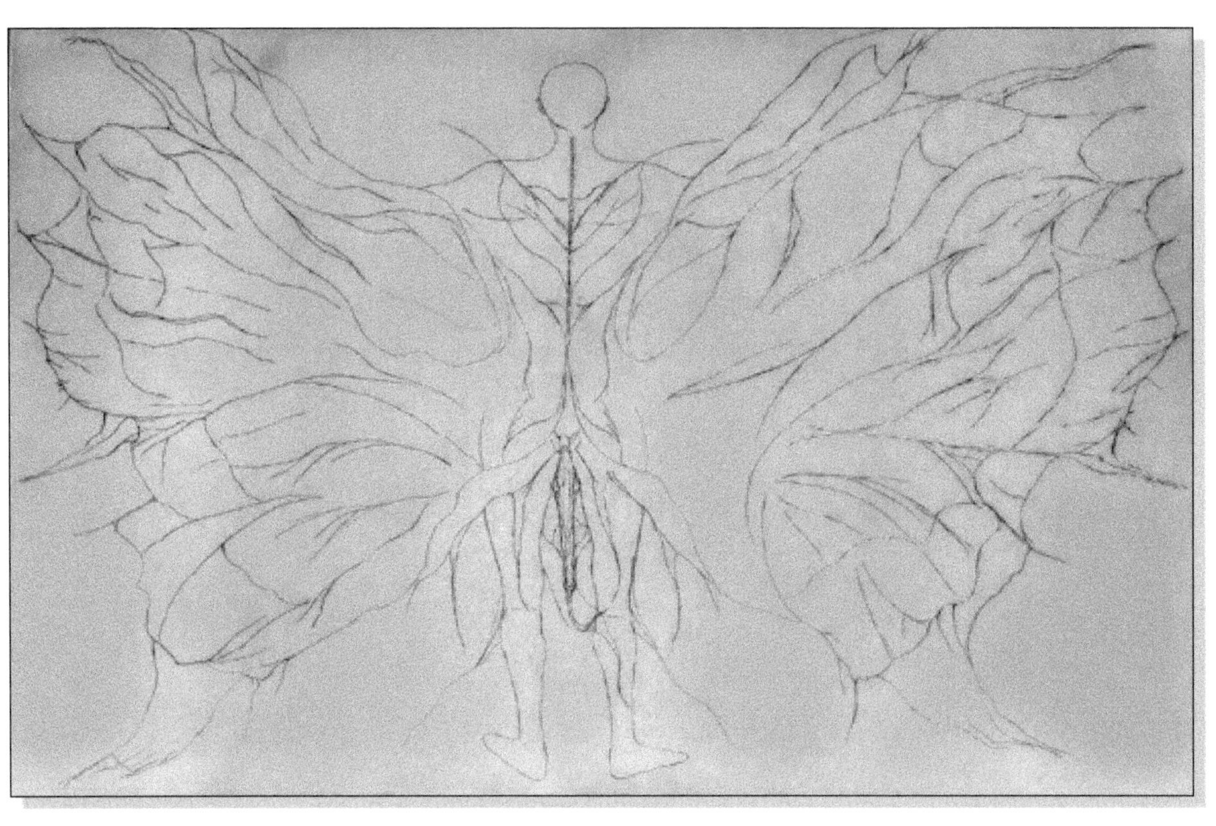

TRAUMATIZED

Traumatized. While in a state of animated suspension, I envision myself being set free.

Recently I found myself numb to what I thought was my reality, awakening later to what was actually going on, paying conscious attention to it.

Because I was numb, my foresight was deadened to that which I thought was a real insight.

Once an innocent child who grew into an adult, I am still left to figure out for myself that life is a holograph, an illusion, and that reality is a boxed-in methodical dream.

Numb, I do not know how to interact with those who cross my path but do not enter my personal space.

My parents failed to teach me about the reality of life. I should have been made more aware. I saw myself falling into an abyss, having no control over the things I was kept sheltered from.

I was not given the keys to life. Otherwise, it would have helped me develop the skills needed to plow through while learning which steps to take to keep myself moving along.

Others failed to groom me and mold me. They didn't give me knowledge. I wish they had planted seeds within me to cause my soul to harvest life experience.

I am learning to let go of the fact that I did not gain the skills that would have helped me move forward more smoothly. I would have better met the challenge to develop inner strength at an earlier age. I was sheltered from the things that otherwise would have taught me life lessons. Now this is my burden, as I still need to learn some life lessons.

I was not shown how to interact with other women, and I wasn't told how these relationships should flow.

Left traumatized, I was an emotional wreck, struggling to understand women, as I was given a false perception of them. I was entirely unprepared for the different stages of life, trying to survive one more day.

I was traumatized and confused, unable to understand why many women rejected their sisters, had no particular discipline, failed to discipline themselves, and chose not to have a family or prepare for tomorrow. They did not understand dating and mating, and they had no idea how to handle their household finances. I could only ask what happened to them.

I remained traumatized when I tried to apply the principles I had learned as a child, realizing that they did not work well for me as an adult. It was a challenge to adapt well to adulthood.

I was left traumatized by women I had admired and respected as my counselors when I was younger. My adult mind became a torture chamber. I thought I had a bond with these women, but apparently I was wrong.

Many women today prefer to have a close-knit circle of friends who benefit them or whom they can manipulate and control. They refuse to perform the duties of motherhood, dis-respecting others' primary relationships by purposefully creating conflict for the couple, leading to chaos and confusion. These women struggle, rejecting principled behavior and choosing not to nurture that which needs nurturing.

Many fail to honor themselves, trading their womanhood for socially preprogrammed behaviors that are weak. These illogical behaviors cause problems later when developing relationships.

Women do not tend to ask themselves why they devalue other women and how they developed such a perception about their own identity. They do not speak about their fall from grace or their mental problems.

I was traumatized once I learned that many women are dishonest and betray each other, also failing to support other women.

I am traumatized when I see the hatred and jealously that runs deep between women, not to mention the ultimate, backstabbing, which causes me to suffer and feel anxious whenever I am let down this way.

Not knowing how to deal with these various things prevents me from steering myself away from these people who rob me of life.

I found myself walking on pins and needles in the midst of every conceivable life circumstance. I was also in a state of confusion. If my parents hadn't sheltered me from the things I needed to learn when I was young, then I'd likely be able to deal with these things better.

The lessons I was not taught when young have left a void that still lingers. I was given an incomplete set of building blocks.

Witnessing the aftermath of the things I've described leaves me shaking my head. I hate to see what some women have become. I have awakened to the life around me. Even with all my mishaps and missteps, I remain standing, making an assessment.

ACCOUNTABILITY

In the candy store the other day, on the shelves, I saw an assortment of candies, including terror candy, horror candy, trauma candy, and drama candy.

I saw on those shelves candy labeled "Abuse," "Ego," "The Hunting of Humans," and "The Endangerment of Animals."

I stood in awe looking at all these things, knowing that if I were to choose any of these items, I would be held responsible for the actions my body engaged in and the thoughts that my mind indulged in when I gave them my attention.

Although I hold myself accountable, I always fight a desire for things I shouldn't have.

I am still learning what would enrich my soul, although my ego is still at war to feed itself.

I see that life's challenges are many, but I will not forgo my responsibility to keep trying.

A MOMENT TO BREATHE

Every time I learn of your wrongful situation, I can only express my sympathy.

I feel your pain; I understand your agony;

I have learned of your false imprisonment, and I have sympathy for your being defeated and for your suffering.

I am angered by your wrongful death. I feel that I carry the world on my shoulders every time I learn of another senseless loss.

Sometimes I need to pause just for a moment before taking the next step to think of the burden of sorrow that human beings carry.

Your pain has become engulfed within my energy. I need a moment to sit down and breathe.

WHAT IF?

Let's speak about the subjects of intimacy and sex and consider how these terms are defined.

Intimacy involves two individuals who are devoted to each other experiencing a growing emotional bond while building a physical connection. Advanced intimacy often grows into a long-term relationship with the possibility of marriage.

An intimate relationship causes a person to grow with many opportunities for showing love and devotion. Some may share that their intimate relationships are sometimes fraught with altercations, feelings of anxiety and sorrow, and breakups and makeups.

Sex is something that people see differently depending on who they are. Some like to have sex without any commitment. This I find questionable. They suffocate themselves with lust without gaining control, or they freely engage in intercourse with anyone who's available.

Sometimes people have sex as if they're making a business deal, leading to scandal or some other unfavorable situation. This is because people think they have control over their romantic entanglements.

I am pointing a finger at anyone who approaches sex as a game. What is the cost of winning or losing with a finger pointed back at you? Did you commit any wrongs or rights? Is there someone you have to answer to?

What about the children born after a casual sexual encounter? Some of these children experience negative aftereffects. Likely half the human population is made up of people who were born as unplanned pregnancies.

There is no right or wrong until a third person gets involved in the mix, or so it is said.

When two people have casual sex together, it sparks unwanted behaviors. The child of this temporary union will likely endure hardship, likely not being welcomed.

Now there is a connection between the spirits of two people who were never intended to share a fate. They were blindsided by the outcome, not having known what it would be when they first walked into this confusing situation. What motivates them is lust, which leads to a downward spiral of setbacks.

The setbacks begin when two people first volunteer for this game of cat and mouse. Their desire to have sex with each other overrides their common sense. They do not know the importance of being responsive.

These people do not know that their temporary desire for pleasure causes them to fail to consider any long-term commitment. It is damaging to use one's own body for a moment of pleasure without any commitment.

What if a person who initially thought he or she was innocently playing falls victim to such a ploy? Seems like the person was just waiting to be played.

What if a person could tell that the person he or she is considering having sex with is a charlatan who will leave after having a few moments of pleasure? A charlatan is someone who has bargaining chips that depreciate in value. Should a person get ready to be a committed partner? If a person *should* know better, then does he or she think to want better?

The two separate, but not equal, entities follow a business model that others want to adopt. What is the value? Free to choose, we may waken an individual to face up to reality. He or she has created a platform that attracts genuine followers.

Marketing intends to shape the minds of those who are hypnotized by it. Becoming transparent could lead to backlash with unfavorable reviews. Admirers should take a stand when the real motives behind the business model are revealed. Another audience member's interface has intervened, introducing a social model to the dark side of the platform, separate but not equal in terms of competitiveness.

The dark side of a partner's platform comes with a fan base. The public as onlookers agree to endorse things of which young people and fragile people should stay ignorant. When walking on the dark side, don't allow these two types of lifestyles to intertwine.

What if this unintended endorsement is for profit only? Companies are selling their products, hiding the truth from misguided souls. This is nothing more than trickery by those who have mastered tricks and spells.

Is a proposed romantic encounter a business decision or a potential love connection? Really, could an inexperienced person know when love is love or when it is just a pretense of love, better left alone? Everyone should know the difference between making a decision and making a love connection.

Perhaps affection and closeness are missing. Know, by studying behaviors, how to determine if the person you are attracted to has an agenda. Get the information you need by using your reason.

If you are engaged in a love connection, first track your experience, then judge the action you've taken, ask for advice, and continually observe events. Advice from others will help you determine if this person will offer you security or not.

What if answers about your own actions are not handed to you but the questions are left for you to figure out?

Should you feel shame when you gain the maturity to make decisions to stimulate your own growth?

Is it right to ride on another's back to elevate yourself? You should know how to act. Wise people know how to make decisions that benefit them in the short term and in the long term.

Should a person feel ashamed for being an opportunist and sabotaging another person's opportunity only to ensure his or her own growth? What if a person's actions are guided not only by self-interest but also by greed?

The negative consequences of any poor decisions made by adults will be visited upon their children. Many of these children will feel angry, waiting for the moment to express their feelings.

When someone is manipulated into having sex by way of tricks or some other method, he or she may have an uncertain outcome.

Surely you have wondered where strangeness in a personality originates. Some personalities lash out, wanting answers, making an assessment of themselves, or citing the judgment of others. What if we were to listen and to observe another's facial expressions but then leave the questions unanswered?

Can one redirect one's experiences so they have no effect on one's future actions? Sometimes I wonder if I could change the past, without asking if I should change myself.

Should we try to erase the actions we have taken in the past? How could we use our analytical ability to assess what needs assessing? How do we develop better judgment to make better decisions?

Challenges that have their roots in the past give us insight into our future, because without learning from that which came before, we will become conditioned to accept our own demise.

What if a person were to be guided by wiser people, such as mentors, and thereby take a more rewarding path? Of course, this is a twofold effort, with the first person providing the wisdom to help the second person grow, also providing the insight to build a stronger foundation.

Those who do not have the benefit of receiving wisdom from others may fall prey to those with a different agenda, one typically unfavorable to someone who desires long-term stability. What if a person learns of the agenda, one that is not in his or her favor, with the resulting wrongful behavior leading to a poor outcome?

What if a person hones in on controlling his or her emotions in the game of winning at all costs? Is it possible to control the emotions that are tied to a game of love, when lust later causes confusion, and where innocent people never master the game, which goes too far, becoming almost a ritual against the innocent?

What if a person playing this game of life needs to learn about the trading post to prevent any backlash? This removes any obstacles that would otherwise present an unwanted challenge. The goal is to reward a person for not wasting time or misspending money.

One's mating years are a time to secure one's later years. What if a young person preserves his or her innocence and purity and uses his or her youth as a weapon to manifest future gains? Because the future is right where a person is standing, interchangeable with his or her past and present.

As advised by those who are wise, one should guard one's youth, seeking guidance, proper training, and the tools to allow one to go the distance.

If you live and behave precariously, you will eventually, if not quietly, tilt toward the wasteful side. Thus, you should reject the attentions of certain people, in favor of a more suitable option. Keep your options open in case an opportunity later presents itself.

What if someone does not learn these lessons when young and as a result finds himself or herself betrayed by a sex partner?

Build and promote your own brand just like a business with the tools you were given at birth. What if what a person or team fails to build today reflects on their actions tomorrow?

What if you were to realize that you represent yourself and represent the brand you've built? Such a realization will lead you to take a stand and promote your business to your audience.

Say another person's business tools are things offering pleasure, therefore marketed to people who endeavor to have casual sexual relationships? We address this business model differently. The two brands eventually clash and force a separation.

When a person in a relationship falsifies who he or she is, his or her true intentions will later be revealed.

What if on one hand a person knows in advance that his or her romantic partner is deceitful but, on the other hand, is blindsided? What if the individual knows now and is ready to take a stand to move forward and move on?

Who are we to blame those whom we do not know? Who are we to project our perceptions of reality onto them? We may have different opinions on the many what-if scenarios. We may point toward those who are to blame, but who are we to judge the reality of another?

We should witness but not place blame. We should not express judgment then take sides. We should not spread gossip. Every time we point a finger at another person and blame him or her for failing, we lose the chance to address our own misguided selves and our misjudgment of the circumstances.

What if we were to take a page from someone else's book and later use the things we learn from that individual as a reference, helping us to navigate our own lives with better judgment?

Do others behave in such a way to make a direct impact on your daily life and the decisions you make? What if you were to take a moment and think about those behaviors in an effort to gain knowledge and wisdom?

What if our parents' sins and wrongdoings provide us with the insight we need to prevent us from committing any wrongs against one another?

What if you were to realize that doing better in every area of your life would carry you for the next several miles?

Do we have the right to judge what we have witnessed? Do we have the right to judge life in all its forms?

Relationships come in many forms, following a path without knowing its ending point. We should note that any children resulting from casual hookups do not have to travel the roads their parents chose to take.

Should we continue to judge others for the lives they have chosen, including their intimate lives and sex lives?

THE EGO KEEPS PLAYING US

Marriage, stepping out, divorce, finances. Whether broken or undefeated, the ego will present itself.

Knowing about people's behaviors before signing a marriage contract, we are not surprised by any outcome, unfavorable or no. None of us are ignorant of the things to come, as anything could play out as a life experience.

No matter how much we try to assure ourselves that we are not the sole controllers of our lives, we learn that the opposite is true.

If you are not aware of your ego, then it will become even more dominant. The ego is always at work, looking out for its own best interests.

When we open our eyes to our lives, we see that we must change those things within ourselves that we blame on others, failing to admit to ourselves that we have allowed our egos to stand in our way.

Will lustfulness and temptation ever come to an end, or will we cave in and forever be challenged by these things?

Why do we do the things that we know will result in dreadful consequences?

The ego will always control the decisions we make about things that tempt us.

The ego is a thermometer that measures the effect on a person's self-esteem of having been indoctrinated into a culture with certain social and spiritual values.

There are so many things that either fuel the ego or deprive it of fuel. All these influences are derived from the culture and its social or spiritual values.

The ego is a hot topic on which to reflect. A human being can be nurtured or have a mental condition marked by delusions, narcissism, or brutal authoritarianism.

The human mind can influence the ego to accept religious doctrine that labels a person as less than human. The egos of kings and other leaders of all ethnicities and races are fueled by guns. Egos run the spectrum, some believing they are God come to earth, and some believing they are slaves meant to be servile.

People do not realize that they are not the trainers of their own egos. Most times, the ego effortlessly controls the mind, leading a person to make certain decisions, although the person thinks that he or she is the one ultimately doing the deciding.

Everyone has an ego. That is what makes us different from each other. But many misjudge the scope of their ego's authority.

Since we all have one, we should agree that the ego does demand our attention.

MEMORY OF BEING TRAUMATIZED

It would be of no use if people did not want to have these conversations, because I have a story about being mistreated by others with cryptic minds.

This is a true story about a terrifying event that took place in an office where I worked. The top executive committed a shameful crime. I have to ask why. Soon came a moment of reckoning.

This son of a mother placed a live rat on a large glue trap, then placed the trap in the corridor. As I arrived for work that morning, the thing quickly caught my attention, scaring the hell out of me.

I screamed for my mother when I realized what was happening. Seeing the unthinkable, my body went into a state of shock. It was dramatic and frightening. I lost control of my legs and was shaking all over, walking in all directions to get away from the captive rat.

I entered the doorway. My right leg moved and then stopped. When I looked down, I saw that the sole of my shoe was above the body of the rat, which was alive and trying to release itself. I screamed, crying out for help.

My scream couldn't have been any louder. Surely an onlooker would have thought that my lungs were about to collapse. My heart was beating wildly. The repeated squealing of the rat was a terrible thing to witness. Indeed, it too was frightened, trying to save itself.

The screaming became unbearable. I looked up and saw my boss laughing uncontrollably but not trying to help me. His secretary was smiling too, both of them refusing to offer me any solace.

Those moments of being terrorized seemed to go on for a lifetime. When I first walked into the office that morning, rushing to get there on time, I was at peace with myself, not thinking much of anything, until I turned a corner and entered the executive office. My office was the farthest from the door, down a long hallway. I was a secretary at the time.

I was happy to have be working with the top bosses. I presented a calm front, keeping my head up and being my usual self. However, this one particular boss seemed not to favor people like me with dark skin, natural hair, and contoured lips. Several times he shared that he disliked dark-skinned people.

A week, a month, or a quarter never went by without my being reminded of his deeprooted dislike for people with dark skin, although he himself was dark-skinned. I got the point in the beginning.

This cruel act with the rat was not the only incident like that. Mr. Dan, one of the top executives, not a man subtle with his ignorance, not only put me at the center of attention because of my dark complexion but also often bullied me about the size of my head and the clothes I wore. He did not realize that he was being undiplomatic when expressing his dislikes.

Mr. Dan's failure to deal with himself often caused others problems, as he ridiculed those people he disliked and acted like a bully, something that he said turned him on. I only wish I had called the law and had them handle this problem. I was unassertive at the time and ashamed of myself for not having the strength to address my concerns.

I stopped fighting myself; I stopped saying what I could have done or could have refrained from doing. I realized that I only wanted to survive, keeping a low profile so I could keep my job to make ends meet. I realized others would not risk their jobs by standing up for me. Otherwise many other people could have been helped.

I realized that one's skin color only matters depending upon the society one lives within. Beliefs have changed little since the 1990s.

There were times when my boss told me to go buy him a cup of coffee and gave me precise instructions: add milk and two teaspoons of white sugar. He was adamant about this, saying he could not stand anything darker than his coffee. He further shared that he came from a higher social class of people in Haiti, which was where he developed his thinking about skin tone.

Sickness was not the only thing this man had to deal with. Indeed, he failed to deal with his own personal matters. He was a classifiable fool and a dysfunctional idiot who showed concerning signs and was clearly calling out for help.

His attacks left me traumatized. So, I finally said, "Enough is enough." It was too much for anyone to deal with. Honestly, I was tired. I remained crippled for quite some time, not even wanting to recall the event.

Saying that I had been traumatized, I reported my boss, only to be told by the union president that I needed to retract the complaint about my boss or else experience some negative repercussions that would surely be visited upon me.

That was a frightening suggestion. Later I learned that the union president and the head boss were friends outside work. Employers should never have the right to abuse employees.

My boss's having put that rat in the corridor left me traumatized. I have yet to get over the pain and suffering. In this case, my boss used the rat as ammunition against me, trying to terrorize me. Think about how you would feel with a rat stuck on a glue board that was stuck to the sole of your shoe, the rat squealing for its life.

Indeed, my boss was not blind to his own ignorance. He eventually realized that I was a human being whom he had chosen to disrespect.

When another office director suggested increasing my pay, this despicable boss replied, "No, she does not need an increase. I am certain she knows how to deal with poverty given the neighborhood she lives in." In the same breath, he said, "I'd rather give a pay increase to the white woman because she has to maintain a different lifestyle."

The rat, the glue, and the shoe were all clinging to my last nerve when I received no response to my call for help. Eventually, the shoe landed somewhere in the office, and I ran in the opposite direction.

When you think of playing a practical joke on someone, think first about whether you might terrorize or traumatize that person. Consider the individual's mental capacity and sense of well-being. Sometimes if you play a practical joke on someone, you end up with a lawsuit being filed against you.

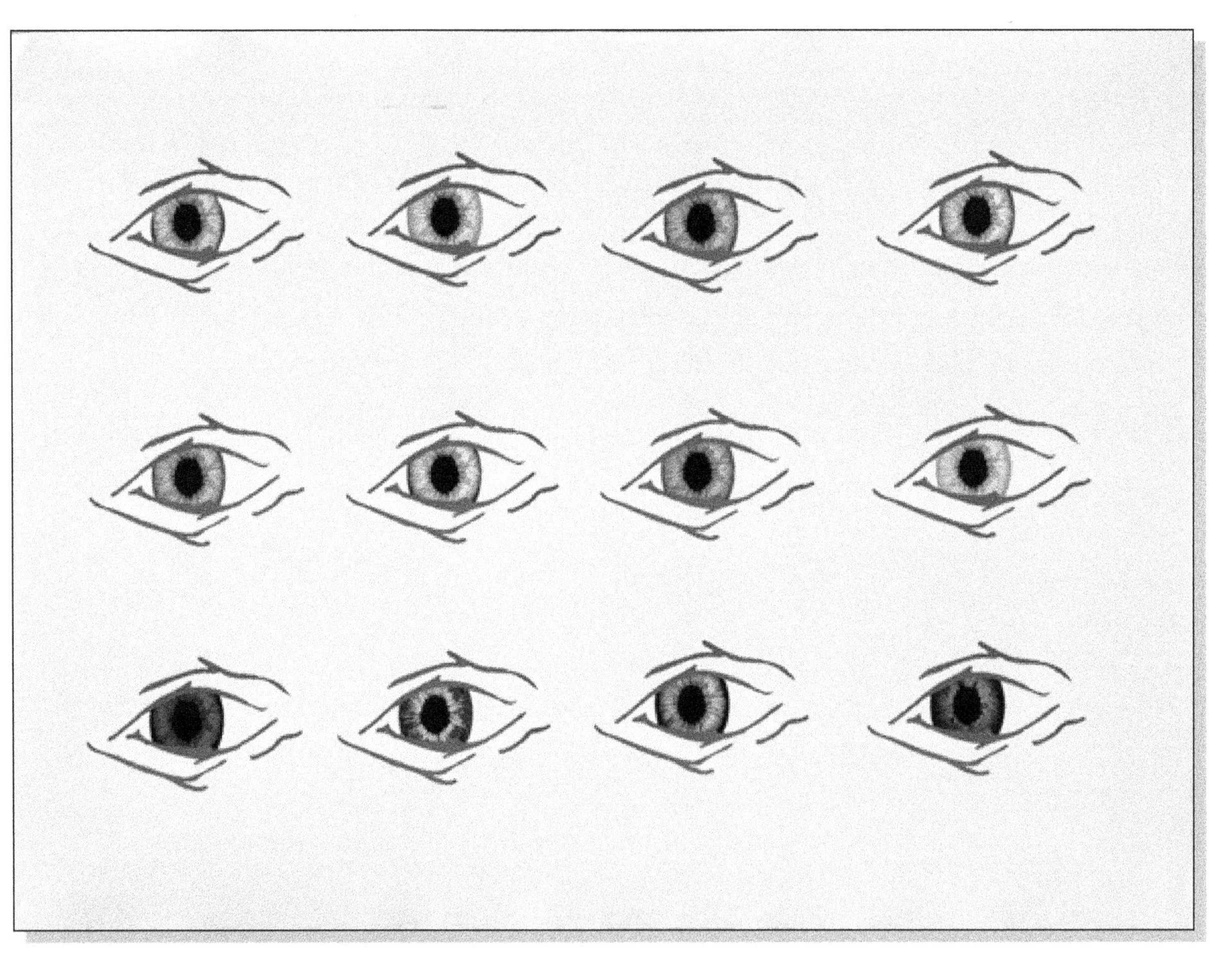

PEOPLE BEING PEOPLE

Everyone is acting like everybody else, and everyone is trying to sell themselves, but not everybody is running after someone else. Most struggle with being themselves.

Someone is looking for something, for that thing no one else will have, while many people are trying to find somebody who will give them a helping hand.

Sometimes people will tell you something they don't want anyone else to know. Sometimes people can't wait to expose something they have learned about someone else without even knowing the person.

Many will turn around and make a mockery of someone, then rush to pass judgment on those things they don't understand, while others keep their eyes on the things that are shared.

One person may know a secret, while another promises not to tell. Others will not keep a secret; they will share it with anyone who cares to listen.

Many will challenge the messenger, and others will stay open to learning, but there are those who will always reject whatever the messenger brings to them.

Some may choose to act crazy, and many may pretend to be sane, but one day those who pretend to be crazy will find themselves functionally insane. However, another's craziness should give a person the ability to see his or her own craziness.

Some people try to be in the know, while others know nothing all, but some don't give a damn about anything and will one day repeat the lesson just to learn those things they should have learned before.

Some prefer to use profanity to express themselves, having mastered this language and choosing to use it every time they speak. Others limit the use of these harsh words, exercising precaution by removing themselves from any situation that would tarnish their names.

Surely anyone who knows anyone else will agree that English is the most difficult language to learn and that it is widely accepted as the language of exchange.

There are those who work as night riders, and many scorn the work they do, but many don't know that those night riders have a list of clients.

Not everybody likes everyone else, and not everybody gives a damn, but those who are fallible should start loving themselves.

Some people listen to others crying about the things they regret, while others sit back and smile, rejoicing, saying, "I told you so," having given the warning long ago.

While sometimes people admit to having regrets for not having learned certain things, some do not admit to having regrets. Life may become more challenging for this latter type if they continue with no intention of learning those powerful lessons.

Everybody pretends to know the things they should have learned, but not everybody admits that they will someday make an adjustment and move on.

Some will preach that they know all they need to know but will not disclose why they don't teach others what they need to learn.

Many look for happiness outside themselves, but not everyone knows of its value or knows that joy could result from a life change. Not everyone can conceive of having freedom and being happy with themselves.

Some know that others will not seek happiness without understanding that one must have values if one is to appreciate things and have gratitude.

It is a tall tale that there is somebody for everybody. Time is running out for me to find my special person.

Nobody will love everyone, but many may journey in search of love. You will not find that particular someone without first learning to love yourself and accepting yourself.

In yesteryears, people took a chance investing their money in a market they had no control of. Some people took the wiser step of investing in themselves.

People gamble when playing the game of life, which they think they can control. Some claim that not betting on another's platform will cause a financial setback because of the imbalanced scales.

Some struggle to learn life lessons. Some keep creating things that no one else wants to own.

Some people may stare at another, not speaking a word, and others stare as an uninvited challenge. Some people may look at another in awe or disbelief, and others will look at the same person and admire what they see.

Some may look upon others in appreciation of their beauty, while others may quickly glance away after seeing the absence of beauty in a face only a mother could love.

Many will stare at another person stone-faced, while others may look at another with disgust. Some people look at others when they think their faces look familiar, while others look at people with dislike and an intention to shame.

Some people may look at another with a snarl, like the growling face of a wolf, and others will give looks of appreciation. Still others may validate those feelings with their own facial expressions.

Not everybody lives life the way most choose to, as there are many in-betweeners who want to know why.

Some people complain about their lives and share their sorrows, but others know to remove themselves from people who seek to remain failures.

Not everybody is knowledgeable enough to repair a broken life, and not everyone cares to learn about the tools they could use to mend what's broken.

Many people have attempted to go back to a time when they had it all. Many wonder if living in the past is worthwhile since the time has passed.

Not everyone understands that merely talking about the things they cannot change poses a challenge to themselves or others to make a difference. Not everyone knows that life is about giving attention to the things that will stimulate positive change.

Everybody has an opinion, mostly expressing things that do not matter, but not everybody uses their freedom of speech wisely. Some people may not understand the power behind their words or know that it is an undeniable right to speak one's mind in public or in private.

Many claim that it's their lawful right to express themselves, while others are assured that freedom of expression has its limitations. Not everyone understands that misspoken words lack power. Perhaps unseen hands are trying to control us.

Some may think that their minds are free to think as they will. Most people never question their freedom to think as they do, while many never bother to think on their own. If a person could think independently, then no one would need to question his or her intentions. For those who remain puzzled about their freedoms, they should keep waiting for the time when this question has grown old.

Minds are corruptible. Evil people who engage in mind control have no moral compass. With more losers than winners at this life game, people never seek to discover if the mind they own really belongs to them.

Many may think they have the freedom to think independently, while others understand the power held by the corporations that control them.

Some may not accept that they never have control over their own minds, nor do they understand that their thoughts have been shaped by those who no longer hide behind a corporation, private enterprise, or government.

Everybody has a body waiting to mature and take shape, but the number of people who market their bodies is determined by the world. Many may study their bodies using the tools they have, while others cannot grasp how their bodies could serve their hands.

Not everyone is lost for not knowing the power of the body, but many fail to master the art of using it purposefully. If the cheapest price is a dollar, and if respect comes with demonstration, then it's up to those who name the selling price of their own bodies.

Many people watch the news each day, but not everyone understands the things they see and hear on the news.

Not everybody cares to extract themselves from the platforms that espouse unhealthy subliminal messages, and not everyone wants to learn about the danger.

If it is time for you to remove those programmed thoughts, know that better ideas will save your mind and secure your life. Few will retreat from stimuli that trigger their sensors, but if saving your own life is not essential to you, at least try to keep the minds of your precious children healthy.

Not everybody realizes the essence of a woman, and not everyone takes the time to understand her journey or her purpose. Everyone should know the value that she brings, being the mother and creator of all living things.

Many will agree that she shows strength when lending support to others and keeping their secrets. Some will agree that woman is the most important of God's creations, the life portal leading others to determine their purpose.

Some women live their lives being misguided by fools, and some become entangled in loose relationships. And although few will go off track in terms of maintaining their life circumstances, there are those who cherish shared moments of honor.

The trueness of a woman's heart determines her glow and her beauty. A woman is the most important part of life, no matter how other people define her existence.

Not everyone understands a woman's being, and not everybody accepts that she remains a mysterious and complicated creature. But her essence and her balance is reason enough for everyone to appreciate her.

Not everyone realizes the real meaning of a man, and not everyone takes the time to understand his purpose of leading and protecting others.

Not everyone embraces that a man is the essence of a powerful warrior, being a soldier, a husband, and a father, exercising his power through his consciousness, which is guarded by his masculinity. A man is complete, as are all others, according to the planetary com-pass within him.

Everyone should know the power that a man has. Some may challenge his strength and question him with distrust. Some will describe a man as being weak and corrupt, asking a whole host of questions that may cause people to examine his intentions.

Others see a man merely as who he is, not analyzing his purpose but accepting his existence.

Many people desire money, but not everybody knows its value. People may not realize that currency these days is merely an IOU with no real value. Others will continue stealing real property from the masses, seeking silver and gold but not realizing that land dominates everything.

Particular people place a value on currency for the masses who make up the labor force, working from sunup to sundown until it's time for them to die, with many being the walking dead.

If people would turn those lies about money into truths, then more would know that they actually have the power to gain capital by controlling things in the natural world such as precious metals, for example, gold and silver. Water is another natural resource needed to sustain life, one of a large number of natural resources.

Some will pretend to be a friend, not revealing their true intentions. Others maintain false friendships by lying, blindsiding their friends on the way to building something supposedly based in honesty.

Some people set an agenda for their friends, something a person could learn about through their connections and by studying their friends' behavior.

Not everyone stands idly by when those who claim to be one's friends are telling lies. Some people do not hesitate to show their true nature, straight up revealing their character.

The people who are most comfortable with letting another person into their lives are those with only a small circle of friends and family. Not everyone will challenge themselves by competing with themselves, instead wasting their energy trying to compete with people who don't care.

Many people ask a lot from others, and some ask for nothing—and to ensure that some get what they want, they lie, beg, steal, or kill.

The present is all we have, so we should live in it. The people who live in the past have got things all wrong.

People may think they have nothing in common with a person from a distant land or a different culture, practicing different customs, including the various daily rituals related to survival. These people should be told that the difference between them and the people who speak a different language is not so great.

Anybody who thinks he or she is someone special and is superior to others should learn to appreciate all the different sorts of people in the world. We should all aspire to respect those differences, while accepting that we function as one unit, being interconnected.

Some may tell stories of yesteryear, whereas others will speak of a promising future. But few care to see the past as a point of reference, refusing to use it as justification for their present condition.

Some allow the past to determine the present, reminding them of what they could be doing today if only … But not everybody understands that today is a reminder that the selves they will be tomorrow are dependent upon yesterday's lessons, even while they're still learning the lessons of today.

Everyone acts like everyone else, and no one goes on a search to find themselves. People will continue to be people, waiting for others to bring about change.

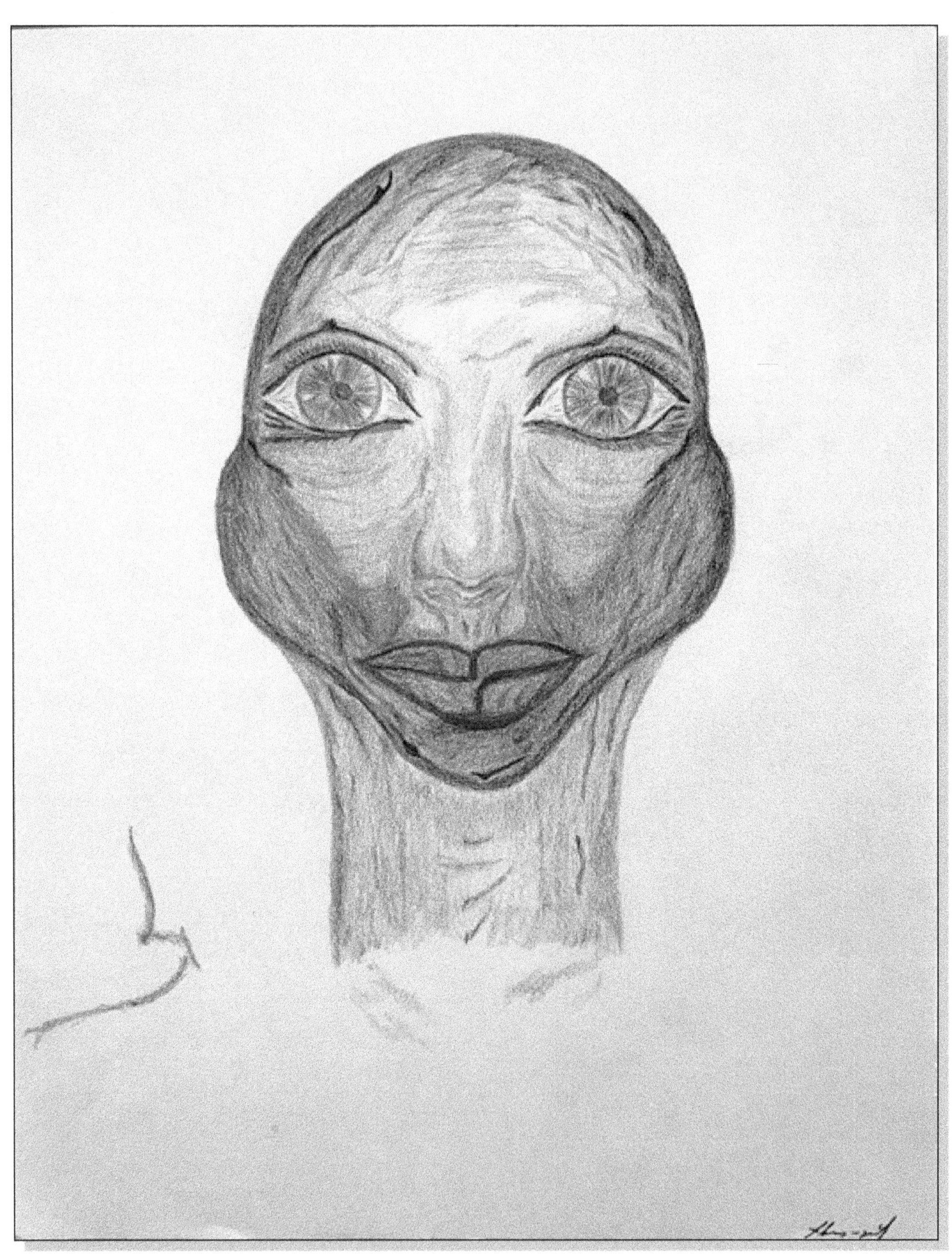

AMERICA THE CONTINENT

Mother Earth shall not cry for her children, for she is here to embrace the essence with an offering of life to support the expansion of creation.

Mother, we speak quietly as the children who were seeded/birthed on this continent, who have connections to the soil from which we came and who are the essence of our physical bodies, but not the whole of our spirits.

Along with the roots from the earth that support the branches of a tree, children are the arms outstretched toward the landmass, the rivers, the creeks, the forests, the hills, and the mountains.

Allow us to capture and shape the different lands, those that remain fertile, and also the wastelands, desert land, badlands, swamplands, rocky mountain peaks, bald mountains, flattop ridges, the Cascade mountains (the Alps of North America), and the alpine hills.

There are the streams in the valleys, along with rapids and rivers. There are lowlands, pastures of grass and weeds, buffalo grasses, prairie lands, and fields of grain.

There are the climatic changes, the crops producing grains, the ecosystems and creatures, the plants (flora), the sand dunes, the natural resources, and the ancient man-made rainforest that was recently claimed, but for certain reasons we shall stick to the rainforest that was originally claimed.

This is where the beauty of the earth lives with its painted soil and red clay found in desert areas. There is also the in-depth beauty of the Painted Desert, found in the Petrified Forest National Park.

The landmass of the United States includes tropics, desert, subtropical and temperate regions, rolling hills, man-made mounds, and the forgotten pyramids.

Let's commemorate Mama for the protection and love she gives to the animals, including the aboriginal animals and those that have been introduced and/or domesticated to serve people and provide for their comfort. Also included are the various species of deer, along with pronghorn antelopes.

We see and appreciate the giant stag, red deer, mule deer, jaguar, bobcat, lynx, panther, mountain lion, black bear, grizzly bear, polar bear, and Kodiak bear. We won't leave out the mountain goats and those bad-tempered wolverines, or the little weasels, stoats, martins, and minks.

There are the many species of ravens and hawks, doves and pigeons, and other birds such as swallows and swifts, blackbirds, red jays, and blue jays, plus some exotic species.

What about the swift movements of those falcons and the swooping eagles hunting jackrabbits?

We acknowledge the bison, coyotes, foxes, golden eagles, alligators, monitor lizards, other lizards, other reptiles, tortoises, rattlesnakes, other snakes, toads, frogs, salamanders, newts, amphibians, squirrels, bats, and various rodents.

Don't forget the moose, the mustang, otters, raccoons, badgers, or seals.

Mama has given us even more beautiful life, including the ocelot, other cats, shrews, hares, frogs, gophers, sloths, skunks, turtles, beavers, and opossums.

There are flying squirrels, groundhogs, prairie dogs, porcupines, and the macaws and Amazon parrots that fly free in the rainforests.

Not to mention the tapirs with their little trunks, crocodiles, llamas, and wild turkeys that live within nature, along with the millions of insects of many types.

Let us speak about the land animals and the marine mammals, including whales. Also fish and beloved domesticated pets, including dogs, cats, and ponies, just to name a few.

But we must not forget our ancestral animals, including the mammoth, camel, saber-toothed tiger, and dinosaur, with dinosaur remains being found in various locations across the Hemisphere of North America's landmass.

We should consider that the animals and birds have much greater intelligence than we believe. They foresee what is to come upon these lands. They may sacrifice their lives to help sustain ours.

North America is known for its uniqueness and its many territories and different states, some remembered as nations, once known as the thirteen colonies, but later forming a union of fifty states. Each of these states is also known by many as its own separate country within the land once known as Turtle Island, as well as by other recorded names.

The animals are like children kneeling at the feet of their mama, showing gratitude for the interconnection of the families. Mama, we keep hearing you cry, seeing that we your children have forgotten the gifts bestowed upon us for our own survival.

Mother, we give thanks for our ability to breathe the air, with the air also supporting our towns and cities, stretching to the inner portion of the landmass.

We hear Mama screaming and calling on her kinsfolk in the United States, asking them to rise up and embrace each other with love and protection.

Mama of our United States, we see your guardianship and the protection you provide for your children, feeding them, teaching them, and sheltering them while nature uplifts them. This land is known to serve its population, although for some that statement may be a stretch.

Mama demonstrates her love from coast to coast, from ocean to ocean, for the people on this landmass, traveling either by foot, boat, or air, honoring her essence and her beauty.

Speaking of the beauty of the peoples, the beautiful North American continent is home to people of various cultures, their heritage connecting them as we hear the flow of the different colorful languages. Remembering those ancient languages nearly forgotten, we across this vast continent (and on some associated islands) share the same customs.

We should appreciate climate change, weather patterns, and the air currents, with one of nature's purposes being to feed all living things.

Let us remember the essence of nature and understand that the currents that help us navigate across bodies of water also allow us to travel to other lands. Not to be forgotten are the many waterfalls.

Although we embrace our brethren and sistren from other lands, we must bring to front and center the mama of North, South, and Central America, including Canada (although culturally linked to Europe), with all its islands and claimed territories. We fight to save our mama's children.

Mother, we speak to you of inhaling an extra breath while gathering the understanding that everything somehow matters, that things are connected somehow.

When hearing those cries, we learn of the lungs being smothered with polluted air. We hear those cries because piles of undisposed trash cause congestion and respiratory ailments, also messing up the terrain, which is begging for cleanup of the garbage and human sewage.

We see people suffering and sick, but some don't care if Mama is able to breathe or if her body will continue to decay from radioactive isotopes in the earth's crust.

We pay attention to Mama's call when witnessing the polluted water unsuitable for human consumption, full of toxic waste. We see Mama struggling to alert us to the danger that others place beneath her children's feet.

Mama, we apologize for allowing others to disrespect your offerings of peace.

Mother, we understand that others disregard the repeated message to stop telling lies about your children's place on the land and to stop causing destruction to the planet. We know that you would like your children to live in peace.

Mama, we heard those messages the first time they were spoken, and we know for the last time that North America is our continent, and it has always been great because nature has harmoniously provided all life, including vegetation, and made plentiful the natural resources. Now the continent suffers from carrying the burden of toxic waste.

We are here today to speak about the pain that you bear and the side effects of chemical waste disasters, the chemicals engulfing the land and the water. Is it needless to report on the defertilization caused by pesticides in the soil?

Our concrete jungles—cities and big towns—make dirty what remains of any clean air.

Let's speak about the wars on the planet that affect all of us, as opposed to peace, which would increase the probability of our living healthier lives.

As we observe our mama cry, we see that she knows of the pain and suffering of her children, and we can only make an apology to her for failing to maintain the forgotten economies we created to exchange goods. We did develop agriculture, with nature providing the nutrients for the crops.

Mama cries after hearing of the abuse people inflict upon one another and the wars humans strike up against each other, with repeated conflicts, chaos, and self-destruction.

Mama, we turn our attention to the animals that have gone extinct and to the near-extinct among the animal kingdom. We hear about the pollution of the seas, the destruction of lake creatures, and the mammals that have been forgotten.

Let us not forget, Mama, about the trees and vegetation destroyed by the fires caused by human beings or the intentional destruction of our habitats. This is what is now causing our concern about inhaling the air. Without the rainforest, our children's generation may see a significant decrease in the amount of oxygen in the atmosphere.

The forest is what produces the oxygen for our children to breathe, putting carbon dioxide back into nature to grow green things.

Mama, we pay homage to your aboriginal children, who cultivated these lands, and to those of other ethnic backgrounds who traveled from afar. We will always be connected to the soil and to the roots, standing up for the truth. We hear the insightful messages whispered to us, saying that the earth is on temporary loan to us, when we are capable of having love enough to provide unconditional support to the ailing earth.

The children take a stand on environmental concerns and engage in conversation to address the needs that need addressing. The children consciously accept their responsibility and will forever embrace all other cosmic beings to whom we are universally connected.

The energy is what resonates within both the proton and the neutron, positive–negative, representative of Mother/Father of the earth. We feel those deep connections with sparks that flicker through our souls, the sparks that initiate life. Mother Earth knows that her children will not fall. They will continue to stand as guardians of creation, moving forward to multiply life so it may go on.

Mama, we are conscious, and we understand. We continue to work on easing the pain and agony that has been with us for too long.

Although we appreciate the visitors who come to our shores, they will not know of Mother Earth's gift of igniting life on these lands for her children, who are enriched by this soil, and who were made from the soil, having been the seeds planted into it.

We cry out loud to our mama, knowing the strength she has to protect her children and to protect these lands.

Mama, if you should decay before our eyes, nothing would be left to sustain us. We could only wait to die, but we will not die. We are to transform and become part of the constant cycle of energy.

Mama, we accept that the Northern Hemisphere of the America continent will remain the land where your children will always dwell.

As the landlord, we give thanks for this life that affords us the ability to breathe, while taking the time to glimpse the beautiful skylines that are like artists' masterpieces.

We will not forget the majestic sunrise and sunset, which have always energized creation, providing a continual balance to enhance life.

The time has come to reconnect to the land that was created for us to live on, then was molded by our hands, thus blending in with all of nature and becoming one with it.

Not another day should pass where we do not teach those in front, and those in between and behind, about our history while dancing around the fountain created by our mama's breath.

Mama of the continent of North America, I apologize for not mentioning all the precious creations, for not naming your vast landmass, for not mentioning the names of the various languages spoken, and for not giving an exact measurement of this continent's landmass.

The names given to certain features of the landscape and certain bodies of water include Mississippi, La Plata, and Great Lakes. And I haven't put a name on climate change or ecology, not that I forgot to mention them as part of the introduction, but we know that all those creations make up part of the North America.

If that which was created ignites cosmic beings, moving them from the invisible to the visible to enable them to experience the physical plane, then those who go against the grain and deny the existence of these beings will soon find themselves removed altogether because of their adverse and predatory behaviors.

After a long wait, Mama, we offer this overdue apology; we understand the enduring pain you suffer from having witnessed the mayhem and destruction brought to this landmass. It is our overstanding that it is not Mama who longs for humanity to take care of her; it is human beings all along who have needed their mama.

WE SHALL MEET AGAIN

As I waited near my casket on the third day of my passing, I witnessed the gathering of my loved ones, showing their grief.

On the ninth day, when I attended my service, I heard three taps on my casket—the signal that it was time for me to part ways with the earth.

I left behind those with whom I shared a life journey, leaving behind cherished memories until I meet them again someday on the other side.

On the other side, we will continue to share the vibrational field of energy, the circle of life and death. This is the process of renovation through rebirth with each functioning to support the other, sharing the same parallel universe (as we never die).

I shall wait no longer in this place of purgatory (expiating/cleansing/purifying) as I continue preparing for my journey. I will have a new assignment, soon to embark upon another life journey.

Perhaps on a future assignment we shall meet again to complete our assigned lessons next to one another and acknowledge our solar (soul) energy in the physical realm, or what some consider to be the continuation of our transformation/creation.

For now, I temporarily leave everyone behind, as it was an arduous task to break away, with the promise that one day they will find the strength to move on, keeping me in their memories as they continue on their own life journeys.

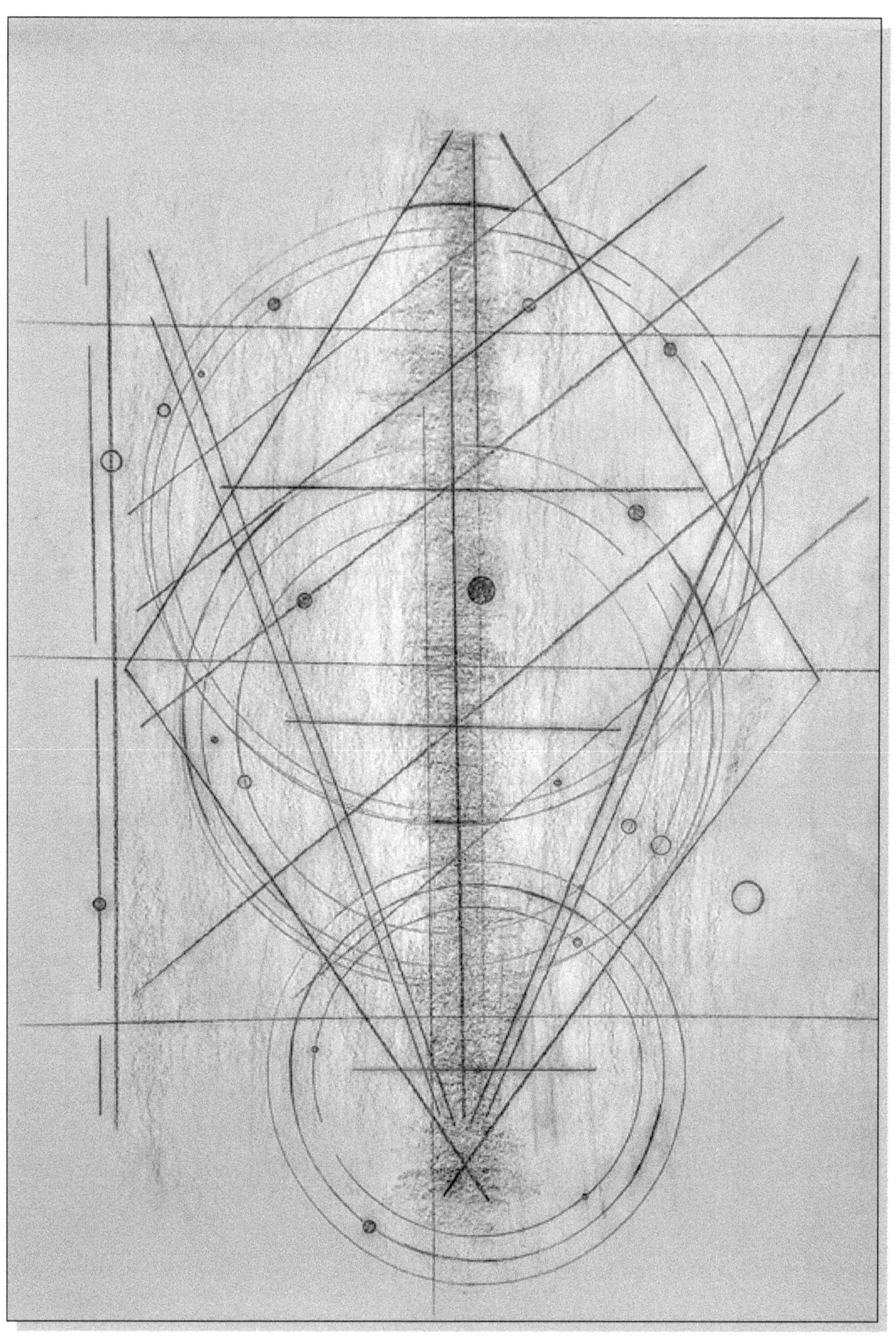

A WOMAN DIED TODAY

A woman died today, and we later learned that she had struggled on her life's journey, never having figured out which lessons she had been assigned. We applied all the facts after her death, trying to digest the reality that she failed to engage with those life experiences.

Life gave her tools, but she declined to empower herself with the knowledge needed to gain the wisdom that would have led to empowerment, self-reliance, and inner strength, which would have helped her grow as a person.

This woman's life was a battle with unsolved problems and demons that haunted her, reminding her of her past.

The neglected love that waited to rear its head showed the broken tracks along her pathway. She strangled herself by not having fulfilled this love. She allowed the thirst for love to remain.

She failed to appreciate the life she had been given, lacking gratitude for those lessons that appeared along her path but that she didn't learn. Subsequently, she forfeited the love within herself that she couldn't see.

The hardship caused by her mishaps kept banging at her tender heart, eventually crumbling her soul. She lost her trail of footprints while failing to learn to love herself.

Her life soon came to a halt. She lost the battle to push herself forward.

The family members and friends who have gathered will never forget the kindness of this sweet soul and this giving spirit. We will join this woman in death once we complete our own journeys.

This woman who died today was a spirit who visited us in the visible world. She will continue to exist in the invisible realm.

MIND AT REST

A moment to escape from the things coming at me. If I had a dollar and a bit of time, I would take each penny from the dollar and write a message for anyone who might pass by.

I grow restless as I wrestle with the belief that one day we will find ourselves in a place without stress and with the freedom to move about while waiting our turns.

I remember sitting on the edge of some lonely porch steps, waiting for someone to join me. I sat swinging my feet and feeling the summer breeze touching me gently on the face.

Those were days when time seemed to stand still, leaving me with nothing much to ponder, no cares, and nothing to focus on. Time just drifted along like it does if it is time that does anything at all.

I heard the wind dancing with itself last evening, and I quietened myself so I could hear it talking. My eyes witnessed the wind dancing and swirling in circles as if whistling. So, I kept quiet, and it whispered in my ear as it paraded around for a few moments on its way past me. I asked for just a little more time to watch the wind blow.

The next day, time awakened me to the sunrise, which embodied the essence of my soul and gave it another boost of energy. I immediately stood erect while paying attention to this force that never fails, giving me another spark of life.

I could be just as free if the breeze would only slow down and embrace my soul for a moment before ascending to go give attention to the next invited audience member.

Let me be the wind that never stays to give rise to indifference. Relieve me of the cloudiness that comes with having made an unfortunate decision and of the unnecessary weight that hinders my thinking process.

I promise to take a dollar and then to take each penny and think about these things. I know I could make a difference and maybe incite change. A hundred pennies will come with a hundred ideas, followed by a hundred creations to serve more than a hundred souls.

I heard the wind passing through in the late evening, and I knew it had come with a message as it whispered softly, brushing gently over my face, speaking clearly that freedom is within reach as it is within my soul, if only I would just believe and pay attention.

Stress eats through atoms, but I will not allow it to control my inner self.

Let any unwanted stress leave, but address that which needs to be addressed. Never leave a matter for another time, but deal with those things that need attention now. Not tomorrow but right now

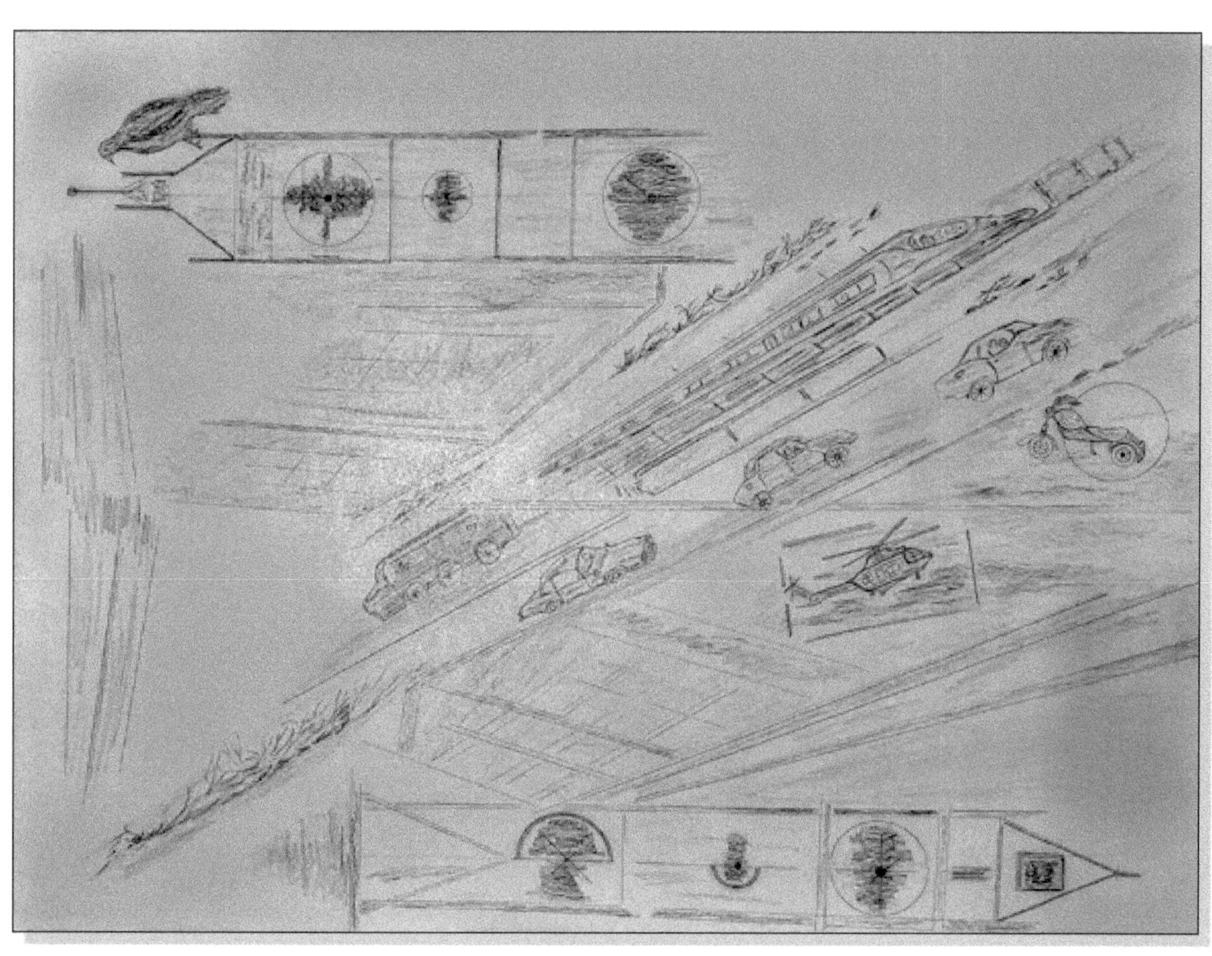

LET'S TALK

A person will see but not will close his or her eyes to that which should not be seen.

A person will listen to that which he or she need not hear.

A person watches and says nothing, although he or she could help out.

A person begs but will not do anything for anybody.

A person shares but never waits for a return, then wonders why he or she is broke.

A person pulls back on the things he or she may need to address and may later wonder why.

A person questions that which does not need to be questioned.

A person sleeps on those things that need an answer.

A person will borrow that which must be returned, but still will not return it.

A person receives a loan that becomes a debt to be repaid.

A person will spend much time talking about minor things.

A person will talk about things that have no value to anybody or anything.

A person complains about things that he or she could change by putting forth some effort.

A person will criminalize another by making a false accusation.

A person slanders another's name, exerting no effort to find out the truth.

A person will keep repeating the same lesson without learning from the experience.

A person keeps denying the truth about who he is, waiting for someone else to tell him who he is.

A person may know the truth but try to run from it.

A person should realize that life is different for everyone and that she can only live her own truth.

A person wrongfully takes a life without knowing that one consequence is that the victim's family now has the right to take his life.

A person soon realizes that her end is near and that a storm is passing through in order to cleanse.

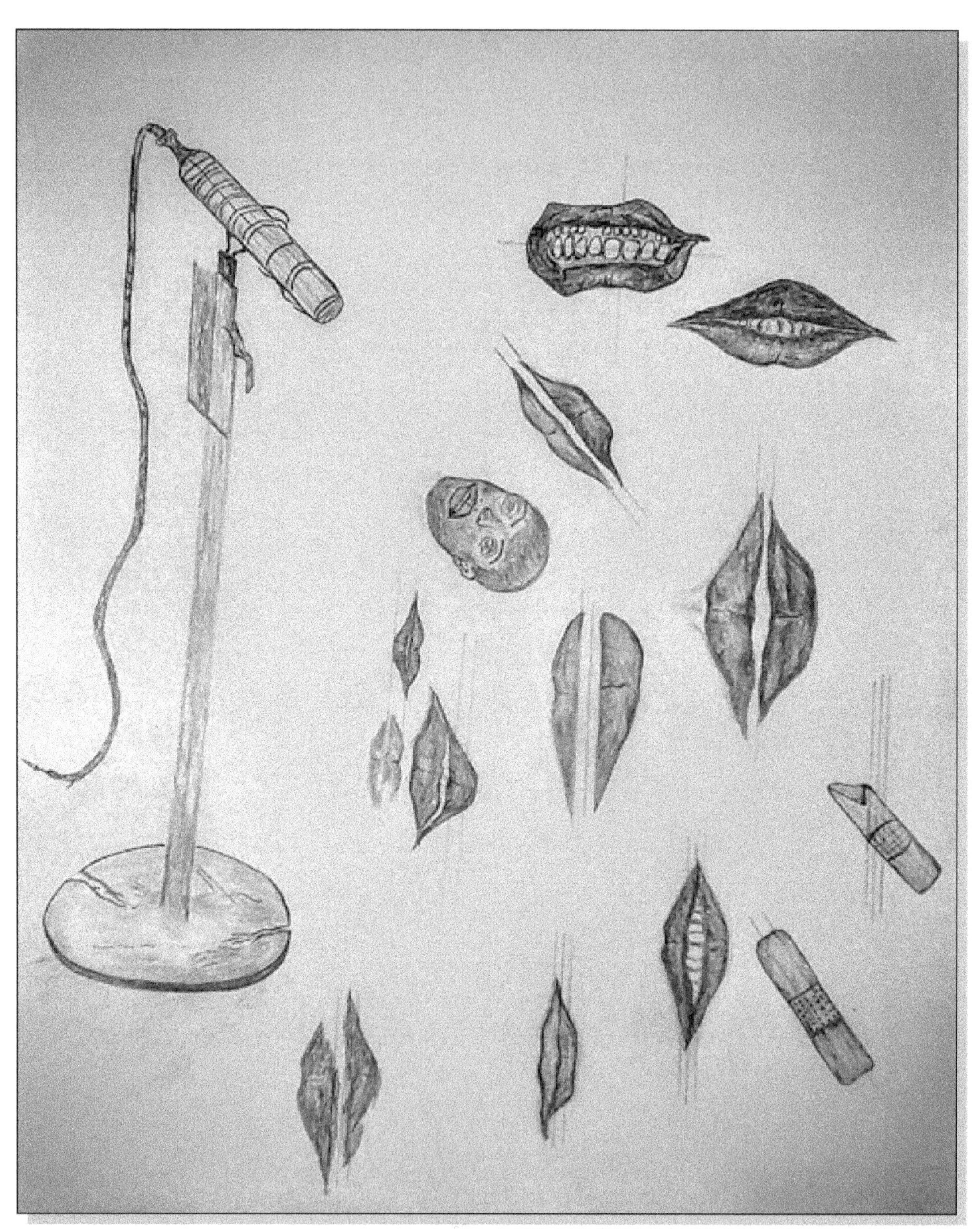

LIFE IS DAMN GOOD

This life is damn good to me, I finally see.

The lesson life gave to me came in the form of chapters, scriptures, and engraved tablets, all waiting to be deciphered.

I walk around with pages to challenge myself, then as I sift through the pages, I see that the situation is complicated.

Sometimes I slip and fall, remaining off balance; other times, I welcome the challenge but fail to learn any valuable lessons.

Sometimes I see things I wish I could unsee, such as the senseless taking of human life. But I acknowledge that the lessons meant for others are indirect lessons for me.

Things come to me in a vision, where I am able to see the future, but the end that I have seen coming is something I will not reveal.

The things in life over which I had control and that taught me lessons enabled me to eventually pass those lessons on to others so they wouldn't have to experience the same things I did.

This life is damn good to me. I analyze the soil and the creatures that live within it, concluding that the life found within requires further assessment. Deep within the soil, I begin to see an image, and the image appears to reflect my makeup, my substance.

Now that I understand the words that I previously misspoke, I deem life as acceptable. I now regret having spoken those words.

Sometimes I dare not repeat an overheard conversation because the words are unjust and opposed to others.

Sometimes I took the wrong path and the wrong steps. Once, I accepted this, but now, who am I kidding? I would like to erase those past experiences.

During one conversation I enjoyed, I shared too much. Had I sat and listened more intently, maybe I would have learned something, instead of overtalking.

When others see me laughing alone, they turn on me and label me as crazy. I respond that I am enjoying some downtime while interacting with my inner self.

Life has been damn good to me, which is something that most fail to understand because they fail to develop themselves and keep out of others' affairs.

I passionately study myself, including how I interact with others, observing their mishaps in failing to rise to the challenges presented to them.

Please do not misunderstand, but I have come to this point in life: I refuse to lend myself to others who complain and cry about senseless things, begging to be validated, talking about their aches and pains, not getting off their asses to do anything constructive, and whining about tomorrow when they do nothing about today. Yes, I decline to entertain their foolish ways of thinking that are sure to invade my inner space.

Life sure is good. I refuse to sit idly by and let life drift along as I waste away.

THE ESSENCE OF TIME

There are no sweeter memories than those of the many colleagues I have known, which I will cherish. I will not forget as I continue following my path.

With a noble spirit, I show my appreciation and gratitude for the many years that I have spent working with my colleagues. Specifically, I appreciate those with whom I have crossed paths and with whom I have spent time.

This journey has enlightened me and elevated my consciousness. It has enabled me to gather the seeds of experience, gain knowledge, and share the wisdom I've been given, which has allowed me to help others and support many people in the community that I have served for many years.

My work as a servant of humanity will continue as I move ahead, hoping my journey takes me around the globe.

Although I will sincerely miss all the dedicated, committed people with radiant energy, not to mention their compassion, at work, and although I will miss all the laughter we shared, I will not forget the complex and challenging work—my case assignments—or the oath that I honored.

Eventually, all things come to an end. Now I am seeing an end to those in-depth reports that I had to take the time to read as part of my duty. I will not apologize for not missing those. Endings are obstacles placed in one's path so that one may figure out other solutions, as there is no challenge without obstacles.

I must give thanks to all those I will temporarily leave behind. I honor you and salute you.

As many of you know, I respect your diligence and your commitment to the job. I crown each of you for staying within the beam of light that made a difference in the lives of those whom we served.

I further give honor by tipping my badge to our colleagues who have since retired, while also remembering those fallen comrades and colleagues who have since become our spirit ancestors. They will never be forgotten.

No doubt, I will remain as an anchor, giving my support if it is ever needed. As I raise my right hand, I promise not to intervene as you continue with your own life journeys.

Many might think that the simply saying of goodbye could turn into an unimaginably long speech. But please remember that from the platform of timeless voices, my position and my purpose, namely, to serve the community, will remain the same.

Following are excerpts from eight of my poems:

Stop running away from yourself. Take the time to discover who you are.

If you don't know the power of thought, then you might never know that you can turn a dream into reality.

You could never imagine who or what you may encounter on your journey through life.

You may never know what talent you have without the circumstances to stimulate its development.

You may never know that your efforts actually helped build up someone else's confidence, empowering not only that individual but also many other people.

Stop letting others shape your reality just because you have neglected to create your own.

Everyone is acting like everybody else, and everyone is trying to sell themselves, but not everybody is running after someone else. Most struggle with being themselves.

Everyone acts like everybody else, and no one is looking for themselves. People will continue to be people, waiting for someone else to bring about change.

Reader, I request that you continue to make a difference. Each day, make a commitment to create a better you, building on your own legacy. Allow yourself to create your own future, organize your present, and record your past.

For now, please pardon my decision to move forward with my life. Know that in my heart, there is stored a colossal volume of memories of my colleagues, with whom I have solid connections. I acknowledge that each of you has given back simply by being you.

Therefore, I thank you for the attention you have given to me. I say in parting that I will see you soon in my follow-up endeavors. I am grateful for the time I have had with you through the years.

The end never comes easily, but it does come.

AFTERWORD

I started writing because I wanted to be heard, then needed to have a voice, then later wanted to share my words. When I first started, I had no plan or direction and no road to start my journey on. I started writing to express my thoughts about my childhood, when I was not allowed to speak freely.

In my early years, I kept all my concerns hidden. After I had been shamed, bullied, and discouraged by adults, I buried my voice, believing that it was a child's duty to stay quiet. Many families believed this. But I definitely was someone who always wanted to know the whys.

So, writing became my form of escape. Writing allowed me to be me, helping me develop myself by digging deep into my soul, where my spirit directed me to keep writing about the things that haunted me. The things that were deeply rooted within me caused me to avoid socializing. I struggled to conquer my fear of people and gain the strength to talk about how I had been abused and the things that concerned me.

Writing allowed me to practice using my voice. It became therapeutic, helping me to heal the lingering traumas of the past. Writing freed me from my self-imposed prison. It enabled me to help others by reaching out to touch their spirits.

When I am writing, I am free from the badgering, the letdowns, the shaming, the criticism—"You're just not good enough," "You are not worthy enough," "Maybe you would do better working with your hands," "You'll likely end up barefoot and pregnant," "If you were just a little more attractive …"—and the hostile gestures, none of which seem to have stopped.

I escape from others' dogmatic opinions and begin creating my own reality, refusing to let those outside take control of me.

I worked on the art of knowing myself. Now, wearing the badge of life, I see that everything I've experienced, favorable or not, has become a tool to use when using my voice and serving humankind.

I never leave my house without a pen and a pad. Each day, my ritual is to write things down, recording every thought and spotlighting every experience to further my healing. Perhaps eventually I will edit these writings and include them in my memoir to lend support to others who are healing.

Thank you, reader, for having taken the time to read *Timeless Voices—Before I Fall Asleep.*

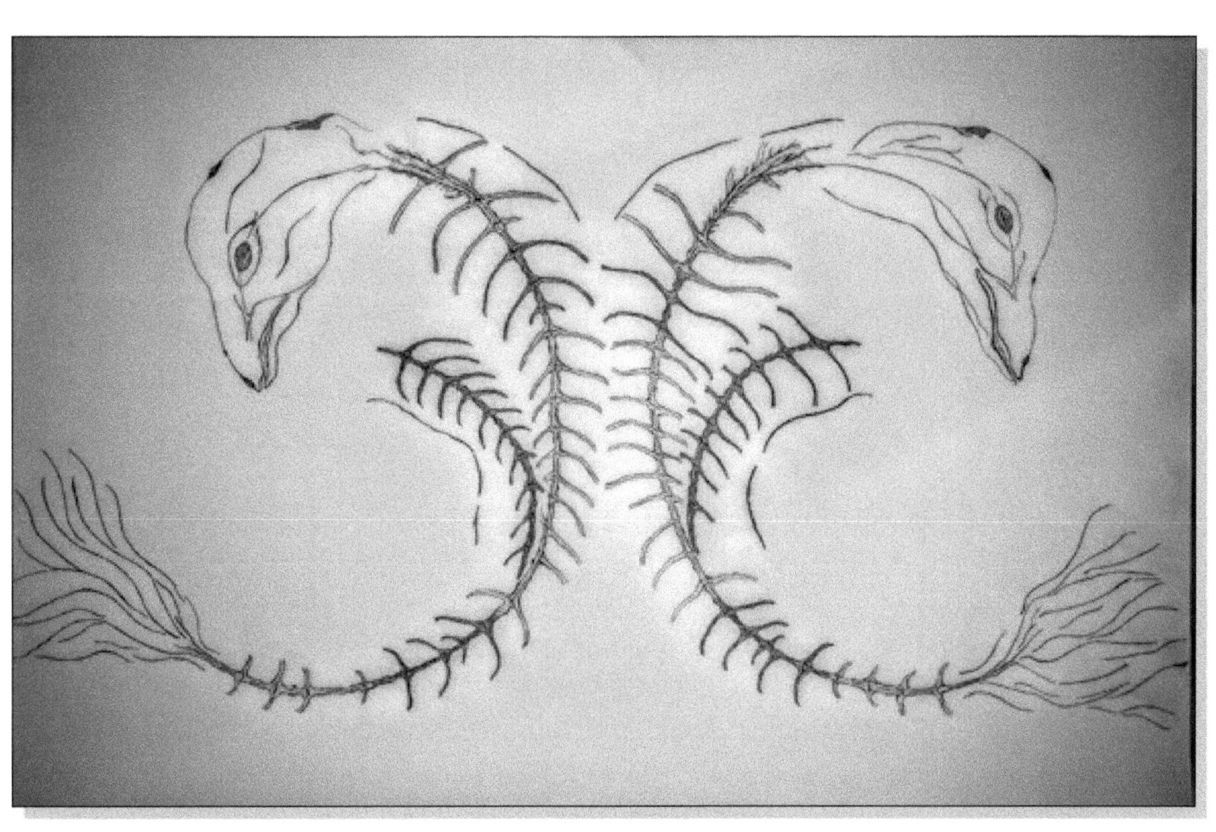

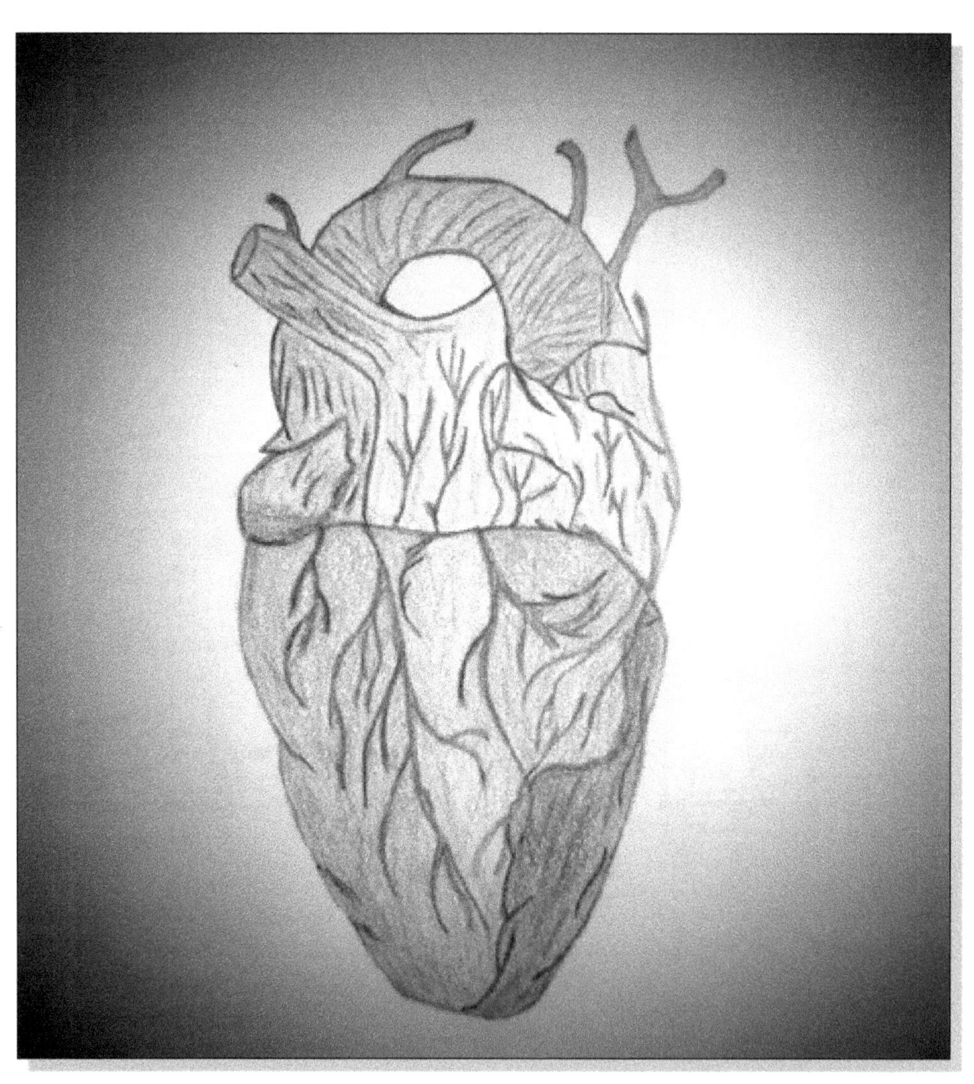

FOLLOW THE AUTHOR

- Website: timelessvoicesusa.com

- Email: timelessvoicesusa@gmail.com

- Follow-up Email: tlvoices@aol.com

- Website: 369.energy

- Email: 369imagine@gmail.com

- Follow-up Email: beforeifallasleep@aol.com

Both websites are accessible on social media platforms including Instagram, Twitter, Facebook, TikTok, LinkedIn, and Pinterest.